A PRINCE
AMONG
Frogs

Books by E. D. Baker

THE TALES OF THE FROG PRINCESS:

THE FROG PRINCESS

DRAGON'S BREATH

ONCE UPON A CURSE

NO PLACE FOR MAGIC

THE SALAMANDER SPELL

THE DRAGON PRINCESS

DRAGON KISS

A PRINCE AMONG FROGS

❧

WINGS

❧

THE WIDE-AWAKE PRINCESS

A PRINCE
AMONG

Book Eight in
the Tales of the Frog Princess

E. D. BAKER

BLOOMSBURY

NEW YORK BERLIN LONDON

First published in the United States of America in September 2010
by Bloomsbury Books for Young Readers
www.bloomsburykids.com

For information about permission to reproduce selections from this book, write to
Permissions, Bloomsbury BFYR, 175 Fifth Avenue, New York, New York 10010

Library of Congress Cataloging-in-Publication Data
Baker, E. D.
A prince among frogs / by E.D. Baker. — 1st U.S. ed.
p.   cm.
Summary: While Princess Millie and her dragon fiancé prepare for their wedding, the
entire royal family of Greater Greensward teams up to find Millie's baby brother,
who has been kidnapped and turned into a frog.
ISBN 978-1-59990-349-1
[1. Fairy tales. 2. Princesses—Fiction. 3. Dragons—Fiction. 4. Kidnapping—Fiction.
5. Magic—Fiction. 6. Humorous stories.] I. Title.
PZ8.B173Pr 2010   [Fic]—dc22   2010004970

Typeset by Westchester Book Composition
Printed in the U.S.A. by Worldcolor Fairfield, Pennsylvania
2 4 6 8 10 9 7 5 3 1

This book is dedicated to my family, who handles
all the horse chores when I get so caught up
in my writing that I can't think of anything else,
and to my fans, whose enthusiasm
inspires me to keep writing.

A PRINCE
AMONG
Frogs

One

illie leaned back against the dragon's side, enjoying the coolness of his bluish white scales on the hot summer day. The dragon, Audun, was curled around her with his head resting on the grass near her feet while Felix, her baby brother, lay on the blanket beside her, cooing at the tip of the dragon's tail that dangled over his head. Millie glanced down when the baby batted at the tail with his chubby hands.

"As far as I'm concerned, the smaller the wedding the better," she said to Audun as she reached out to stroke the baby's red gold curls. "I want it to be intimate, with just us and our immediate families."

"Don't you want our friends there, too?" Audun asked.

"Well, yes, of course, at least our closest friends, like Zoë and her parents and Ralf and his parents and your friends Frostybreath and—"

"Do you see what I mean? It's going to be nearly impossible to have a small wedding. I don't have a lot of relatives, but I do have lots of friends I want to invite."

"Speaking of relatives," said Millie, "I'm not sure what to do about my father's side of the family. My uncle, Bradston, is all right, but I've told you how much my grandparents hate dragons. They can't even accept the fact that *I* turn into a dragon. I can only imagine what they'll say when I tell them about you!"

"Millie!" called her mother, Emma, from where she was kneeling in the garden, supervising the weeds that were pulling themselves out of the ground. "Don't let the baby put that thing in his mouth! You have no idea where it's been. No offense, Audun."

"None taken," the dragon replied, moving his tail out of the baby's reach. Felix began to fuss, so Audun pulled a golden chain from around his neck and held the dangling amulet over the baby. "Here, you can play with this instead." The ice dragon council had given the amulet to Audun to allow him to breathe underwater, and the rolling waves that decorated it soon caught the baby's eye.

Millie's great-aunt, Grassina, sat back on her heels and wiped the perspiration from her forehead. "When we finish this, I'm going to add a new section to the garden. I want to have plenty of fresh flowers for the wedding," she said, smiling at Millie.

"We have to invite all the dragons who helped us, too, you know," Audun said, nudging Millie's foot with his chin.

Millie turned her head to watch Grassina gesture, making a strip of ground crumble until it was well worked and ready for seeds. The seeds flew from the witch's hand, burrowing into the soil. Another gesture, and a dozen willow wands pushed into the soil beside the seeds and wove themselves into a delicate fence.

"Like who?" Millie asked Audun.

"King Stormclaw, for one. If he hadn't given us permission to marry, we wouldn't be having this discussion."

"That's true . . . ," Millie said.

"And then there's his council . . . ," said Audun.

"His entire council?" Millie said, sitting up abruptly. A lock of her long blond hair had gotten caught around one of Audun's scales, and she winced when it yanked at her scalp.

Audun moved his back legs, and his tail twitched closer to the baby. "My grandmother is one of the members, and they all voted to let us get married."

Millie sighed as she reached back to free her hair. "I suppose we'll have to invite them, too, but we can't include everyone we know."

"I didn't say we had to. I just want—YOW! Watch it, kid. Those scales are attached, and I'd like them to stay that way!"

Millie giggled. Her baby brother was just an infant, but his tiny fingers were already strong. She adored the little boy and was still surprised and delighted that he had become part of her life. Although most royalty relegated the care of infants to nursemaids, Millie and her parents spent as much time with Felix as they could. When Emma and Eadric were busy with the demands of the kingdom,

Millie often visited the nursery on her own. Sometimes she felt almost as if she were the baby's third parent.

"Excuse me," Audun said, edging away from Millie as he got to his feet and put the golden chain back around his neck. "My back is getting stiff. I think it's about time for a change." Like the air above a sun-heated boulder on a hot afternoon, the air shimmered around Audun as he turned from a dragon into a young man with silvery white hair and vivid blue eyes. He was handsome whether he was a human or a dragon, with a strong chin and prominent cheekbones.

When Felix's smile melted away and he began to fuss, Emma looked up from the growing pile of weeds and muttered under her breath. Butterflies flitting around the garden rose above the blossoms and flew to where the baby lay. The multihued cloud descended over the baby, fluttering just out of reach of his flailing fists. Felix chortled and his smile returned even brighter than before.

Audun had just taken a seat on the blanket when the shadow of a large bird passed overhead. Millie glanced up. Her heart rate quickened when she saw that it wasn't a bird at all, but a witch with long white hair whipping behind her as she darted to a landing on her broom made of palm fronds tied to a stick.

Millie was used to visitors arriving at all hours of the day and night. Her mother was the Green Witch and in charge of dealing with the magical issues in Greater Greensward. Because Emma was married to Eadric, crown prince of

4

Upper Montevista, she had to watch over that kingdom as well. Witches, fairies, and normal humans were always stopping by to tell her about yet another problem. Millie wouldn't have minded if their arrival didn't usually mean that her mother was going to be called away once again, leaving Grassina and Millie to deal with whatever problems might crop up in the two kingdoms. So far Grassina had been able to deal with it all, but there was always the chance that Millie would be called upon to help, and that the small amount of magic she was able to use wouldn't be enough.

Millie tried to stay calm as the visiting witch, who appeared to be nearly ninety, hopped off her broom like a spry sixty-year-old and brushed her snarled hair back from her face. She was a pretty woman with tanned, not-too-wrinkled skin. When she spoke, her voice was unexpectedly husky. "Which one of you is Grassina?" she asked, peering at the women. "My eyesight isn't so good anymore."

Grassina stood, dusting off her hands. "I'm Grassina, and I know who you are, Cadmilla. How can I help you?"

"You can offer me a drink and a seat in the shade," said the witch. "I've been on that pitiful excuse for a broom since yesterday, and my joints ache worse than a whale with a sick belly." She sighed and shook her head. "Listen to me. I've spent so much time with those old crones on the island that I'm beginning to sound like them."

While Grassina hurried into the cottage, Emma helped Cadmilla to a bench under the spreading branches of the oak that grew at the river's edge. "I must be a sight," the old witch said, fussing with her sleeves as she made herself comfortable. "I got caught in the rain yesterday. It took forever for my clothes to dry out."

Grassina emerged from the cottage, carrying a large tankard. "Why were you looking for me?" she said, handing the woman the drink.

Cadmilla took a long sip. "I didn't want to come, and I wouldn't have if the old biddies back on the island hadn't left me the short straw. I think they cheated and used magic to make their straws longer. I would have, too, if I'd thought of it soon enough. I came because of that sea monster. Wrecked our cottages and drove us into the woods. The ugly beast won't leave us alone. It's been coming for a week and hasn't shown any sign of leaving."

"If you and your friends are witches, couldn't you have gotten rid of a sea monster on your own?" Audun asked.

Cadmilla curled her lip in exasperation. "Don't you think we tried? But either our magic is getting as feeble as we are, or the monster is stronger than all of us put together. All our spells and potions didn't affect Old Warty one bit. That's what we call it, because of its warts."

"And you came here because . . ."

"We heard that Grassina had taken it upon herself to get rid of all the monsters around that town Chancewood . . . Chanceworld . . . something like that."

"Chancewold," said Grassina. "Tell me about the monster. What does it look like?"

6

"It's gray and has a floppy body like a half-empty bladder covered in warts. It stays in the water most of the time, but when it does come out, it crawls around on three big flippers. It has long tentacles with leaf-shaped tips, and it smells like a slop bucket that hasn't been emptied for a month."

"That's one of mine, all right," Grassina said, frowning. "I guess I won't be able to work on the garden after all. If you'll excuse me, I need to get ready to go."

"I remember that monster," said Emma, placing her hand on her aunt's arm. "I'm the one who sent it away. If anyone should deal with this, it's me."

"Don't be absurd. I created the monster, so I'll take care of it."

Emma shook her head. "You can't go alone. I'll go with you and—"

"You'll do no such thing. Haywood will go with me. You're the Green Witch and your responsibilities are here in Greater Greensward. Don't worry. I've dealt with many monsters over the last few years. Haywood and I will be back before you know it."

Although Emma didn't look happy, Millie relaxed and gave an unconscious sigh of relief. She didn't mind helping her mother if she needed it, but then her mother very rarely needed help. All Millie wanted to do was plan her wedding; with her mother there, she just might get the chance.

7

Two

efore she met Audun, Millie had thought she knew everything there was to know about being a dragon. But after they fell in love and Audun had had to earn the right to learn how to be a human, she discovered there were a lot of things she didn't know. Most of them, like how ice dragons differed from fire-breathing dragons, were interesting, but only a few affected her directly. Her sweet tooth was one such discovery. She'd always thought it was part of her human side, so she'd been surprised when Audun, who had been a dragon at the time, nibbled a honey-laced confection and declared that it was the best thing he'd ever tasted. It had never occurred to Millie to try anything sweet as a dragon, but when she did, she discovered that dragon taste buds amplified the flavor so that her entire mouth tingled. After that, Millie got in the habit of fetching a huge bowl of porridge in the morning, dribbling a generous serving of honey over it, and taking it back to her chamber to eat. She was sure most of the other inhabitants of the castle would find it disconcerting to see a dragon eating breakfast in the Great Hall, and she didn't want to have to explain why she turned into a dragon just to eat breakfast.

She was in her chamber eating her porridge on the second day after Grassina's departure for the tropical island when she heard a knock on her door. Thinking that it was Audun, she left the bowl on the floor and shuffled across the room, keeping her wings tucked to her sides so she wouldn't knock anything over. Opening the door, she was surprised to find her grandmother Queen Chartreuse waiting on the other side.

After one glance at her granddaughter, the queen pursed her lips in disapproval. "Can't you refrain from turning into a dragon at least for one day? And if you can't restrain yourself, I wish you wouldn't do it inside. This castle was never built for creatures with your . . . bulk."

"Are you saying I'm fat?" Millie asked, backing into the room. Unlike her mother, Millie had never balked at speaking her mind to her grandmother.

"I'm saying that I'd prefer to talk to you while you're a human. There," said the queen as Millie obliged her by changing form. "That's better. Some people have come to see your mother. If you'd been eating in the Great Hall as you should be, you would know that she was called away to speak to a herd of centaurs who have been stealing horses from local farms. They call it liberating them, which is the silliest thing I've ever heard. Your mother had just left when these people came to see her. Ordinarily, I would send them to see Grassina, but she's away, as you know. Your grandfather and your father have gone hunting, leaving me to deal with everything, but I put my foot down when it comes to dealing with something like this. You're going to have to talk to them, so wipe the porridge off your chin and come with me."

"Who are these people?" Millie asked, following Queen Chartreuse down the corridor. Her stomach was beginning to clench—not a good thing when it was full of porridge. She doubted that she'd be much help in a magical way, and she dreaded telling people that she couldn't do anything for them.

"Fairies! Young people like you have no problem talking to them because you're used to it, but when I was a girl, they never came to visit the way they do now. And I'm not like your father's mother, Frazzela, who dotes on fairies. I have no idea what to say to them. Then there's the wing issue. If they have wings, I try not to stare at them, but I know I will anyway, which is rude. And if they don't have wings, I wonder why not—I always do—and then I lose track of whatever they're saying. They shed fairy dust, too, which is so untidy. Now you go on ahead," the queen said as they reached the bottom of the stairs. "You'll find them just outside the door leading from the Great Hall into the courtyard."

"No one invited them in?" asked Millie.

"Of course not," the queen said, wrinkling her nose with distaste. "You'll see why when you meet them. Oh, and by the way, you *have* gained a few pounds lately. You really must cut back on the sweets."

Three fairies were waiting by the stairs in the court-yard, looking as if they weren't sure they should be there. They turned to face Millie as she reached the bottom step. She'd met the fairy dressed in the soft green gown and matching floppy cap before. Moss had visited her mother and even come to some of the parties at the castle, but the other two fairies were unfamiliar.

"Good day, Millie," said Moss. "Is your mother, Princess Emma, here? We have a problem and we think she's the only one who can handle it."

Millie shook her head. "She left this morning and I have no idea when she'll be back. Maybe I can help," she added, more because she thought she should than because she wanted to.

"You can if you're as powerful a witch as your mother," said the fairy with the pale skin and gown made of shiny green leaves. The nostrils of her thin, arched nose flared when she looked at Millie, giving the fairy's narrow face a scornful expression.

"I'm sorry, I should have introduced my friends to you," said Moss. "This is Poison Ivy, and this is Trillium," she added, indicating the shorter fairy with dark red hair that hung down her back almost to the ground. Her flower-petal dress was only a shade or two lighter than her hair, and it glistened as if sprinkled with dew.

"It's nice meeting you," said Millie. "But I'm not a witch."

11

"I knew coming here was a waste of time," Poison Ivy said, tilting her head back so that she looked down at Millie.

Taking a deep breath, Millie tried to tamp down the irritation welling up inside her at Poison Ivy's rudeness.

Trillium sighed and said in a whispery soft voice, "Perhaps we should go."

Millie started to agree with her. If the fairies thought they needed powerful magic to deal with their problem, Millie probably couldn't help. Aside from her dragon magic, she had very little magic of her own. She could find lost items, but only if they were things she used all the time and had lost recently. She could turn the pages of a book with the wave of a hand, but only one at a time. She could even blow out a candle from across the room, but she couldn't light it again unless she turned into a dragon. Millie wanted to tell the fairies that they'd have to return when her mother was home, but then she glanced at Poison Ivy again and knew from the curl of her lip that the fairy expected her to back down. The irritation she'd felt before flared into a spark of anger.

For most of her life, before Millie had learned how to control her temper, she turned into a dragon each time she got angry. Even now, controlling her temper wasn't always easy. She knew that if she let little things bother her, even the smallest spark of anger could flare into full-blown rage. Millie glared at the narrow-faced fairy, then purposefully turned toward Moss. "If you tell me what the problem is, I might be able to help."

12

Moss shook her head, and her cap slipped down over her eyes. She pushed it back with a rueful smile and said, "That's very nice of you to offer, but I don't see how you can possibly help us. It's a plant problem, you see, and not a nice plant, either."

"Is it one of your plants?" Millie asked, glancing from one to the next but letting her gaze linger longest on Poison Ivy.

"Don't look at me!" Poison Ivy declared. "My ivy has nothing to do with this. I only came along to help."

"There's no need to act defensive," said Moss. "I'm sure Princess Millie didn't mean anything."

"Ha!" said Poison Ivy.

"It's not one of our plants at all," whispered Trillium. "It's a plant so nasty that it doesn't *have* a fairy to watch over it."

"That's right," said Moss. "No fairy wants anything to do with it. It's new to the enchanted forest. We think some horrid person brought it here to stir up trouble. Thank goodness there's only one."

"It comes from a rain forest far away," Poison Ivy added. "Too bad it didn't stay there."

"What's so awful about this plant?" asked Millie. She was intrigued now. A plant couldn't be that bad, could it?

"What plant?" asked Audun as he descended the steps behind her.

"Are you a wizard?" Poison Ivy said, looking Audun up and down. "Because we could really use a good one."

"This is my betrothed, Audun, and he's not a wizard."

"Even so, I'm sure we can deal with a plant," Audun told them.

Poison Ivy snorted. "Not this plant!"

Trillium tugged on Poison Ivy's sleeve. "We could show it to them," she said in a voice so soft that Millie had to strain to hear it.

"I'm not sure . . . ," Moss began.

"Why not?" said Poison Ivy and sneered at Millie. "I'd suggest that you follow us on your broom, but you're not a witch, so—"

"Would a magic carpet do?" Millie asked, anger building inside her again. "I'll be right back."

She left Audun talking to the fairies while she went to her chamber to fetch the carpet her mother had given her for her last birthday. It was also an excuse to leave the fairies for a few minutes. Generally, the only people who were rude to Millie were those who didn't know either that she was a princess or that she could become a dragon at will. Moss had mentioned in Poison Ivy's presence that Millie's mother was a princess, so it couldn't be that. However, there was a good chance that Poison Ivy might not know about Millie's dragon side; Emma had been using magic for years to keep it a secret. Millie was tempted to turn into a dragon to show the fairy just whom she was dealing with— which was exactly why she couldn't let herself do it. Once she was a dragon, the temptation to fry Poison Ivy would be hard to withstand.

The magic carpet was right where she'd expected to find it—buried under all the things she had tossed into the back of the storage room. She pitched the old shoes to the other side of the room and set the broom she'd never been able to fly next to the basket of toys she'd loved when she was younger. Maybe she'd give a few of the toys to Felix.

And then there were all the things she kept because she was sure she would need them someday: her great-grandmother's old chipped scrying bowl; the bouquet of crystalline flowers that her great-aunt, Grassina, had given her and that Millie had broken with one accidental swipe of her tail; the troll-hide trunk that her mother had wanted to throw out; her great-aunt's old magic mirror. Millie had propped the mirror against the wall to keep the magic carpet from unrolling, but the dark wood frame was so heavy and awkward to move that she considered getting someone to help her. Instead she turned into a dragon just long enough to lift the mirror aside as if it weighed nothing at all.

She would have remained a dragon long enough to carry the carpet out of the room, but she was too big to turn around in the small space, so she had to change back into a human. When she was finally able to drag the narrow carpet into the center of her chamber, she spread it out on the floor and sat down in the middle with a sigh. This was not at all how she had meant to spend her day! Now all she had to do was remember the magic words to control the carpet and she could take care of this silly errand. The fairies were worried about a plant, for goodness' sake. Even she could handle a plant!

Because Millie didn't have the kind of magic to control a carpet herself, her mother had given it a simple set of commands. All the princess had to do was repeat a few words and the carpet would go wherever she wanted. It wasn't as much fun as flying in dragon form, but there were certain places where a royal princess would be welcome whereas a dragon would not. Her parents had made her promise never to leave Greater Greensward in dragon form unless another dragon accompanied her. Too many people feared and hated dragons, and she wasn't safe outside her own kingdom. Millie never even flew to Upper Montevista as a dragon. The royal archers still shot at dragons that dared to fly near the castle, which didn't bode well for relations between Millie's Upper Montevistan grandparents and her future in-laws.

"Rise and leave!" Millie said, bracing herself because she expected the magic carpet to levitate. When nothing happened, she tried again. "Climb and depart!" The carpet remained motionless on the floor. It had been many months since Millie had used the carpet. She knew the phrase her mother had chosen was short and to the point, but that didn't help if Millie couldn't remember the words. "Float and flee!" "Ascend and fly away!" she said to no avail.

"I can't believe this!" she declared out loud. "All I want to do is make this carpet get up and go!" The carpet lurched into the air, sending Millie toppling onto her back. Flinging her arms wide, she grabbed hold of the edges and held on while the carpet shot through the window, only to hover two stories above the ground. "Ah," she murmured. "I think I remember it now."

The magic carpet wobbled beneath her as Millie sat up and looked around. She hated that things like this happened whenever she tried to use ordinary magic.

Millie shifted her weight the way her mother had shown her, making the carpet change direction. She straightened her clothes as the carpet floated around her parents' tower and into the courtyard outside the castle keep. The fairies were still there talking to Audun. Though Moss and Trillium both looked worried when they saw her, Poison Ivy only managed to look smug. "So you did come back," the fairy said as if she'd tasted something nasty. "I thought you might have been frightened into running away."

"I'm sorry it took me so long," Millie replied, turning to face Moss and Trillium, "but it took me a while to get my carpet out of storage. Audun, if you're ready . . ."

Millie leaned forward and the carpet drifted to the ground, allowing Audun to climb on behind her. He gave her a searching look as he sat down and crossed his legs. After all they had been through together, he was attuned to her moods more than anyone and often seemed to know just what she was thinking.

"This should be fun," she said over her shoulder, giving him an encouraging smile.

17

Audun nodded, although his eyes showed that he didn't believe she meant it. She'd told him many times how worried she was about her lack of nondragon magic and how ineffective she felt in a family where most of the women were witches.

"Then let's go!" Poison Ivy announced. The next instant she was no bigger than Millie's little finger and sported iridescent green wings. She was the first to dart over the castle wall with Trillium only a heartbeat behind her.

"I'll show you the way," said Moss, and then she too was tiny.

Millie had never flown with fairies before. By the time the carpet rose above the walls, both Poison Ivy and Trillium were out of sight. Moss was careful to stay where Millie could see her, however, although she had to circle back if Millie and Audun didn't move fast enough. Soon they landed in a small clearing in the heart of the enchanted forest.

"Where is this plant?" Millie asked, looking around her as she climbed off the carpet.

"It's a tree, actually," said Moss, settling on the forest floor a few feet away. The air shimmered as she turned back into a full-sized fairy in time for her to raise her arm and point. "It's down that path. Just look for the tree with the red berries and the dead bird by its roots."

"Aren't you coming with us?" Millie asked, feeling a touch of unease.

"We wouldn't go near that thing for all the pollen in the kingdom!" said Poison Ivy, who was already back to full size. "It's up to you now. We just wanted to make sure that someone came to take care of it. Come on, Trillium, I hear they have a new batch of dandelion wine at the old stump."

Moss shook her head as the other two fairies darted away, tiny once again. "I'm sorry, but she's right. We're not able to go near that tree safely. Thank you so much for coming. We weren't sure that even a strong witch like your mother could handle this. Let us know how it goes!"

The air had begun to shimmer around her when Audun called out, "Are the berries poisonous?"

"Maybe," called Moss, her voice becoming fainter as she shrank. "I don't know. But it's not poison you have to worry about." And then she was gone, leaving Millie and Audun alone in the enchanted forest.

"What do you suppose is wrong with this tree?" asked Millie. "What could be so awful about it that no fairy will claim it?" Now that Poison Ivy was gone, Millie's temper had cooled and she started to wonder what she'd gotten herself into.

"Is that what they said?" said Audun. "I thought every plant had a fairy to watch over it. It must be pretty serious if none of the fairies likes it."

"Maybe we should go back," said Millie. "The fairies said this would take really strong magic. My mother should be home soon and we can bring her here, now that we know where to come."

Audun frowned. "You shouldn't second-guess yourself, Millie. There's no need to worry. We're dragons. We can handle anything. Unless it's your human side speaking now, in which case—"

"Are you implying that my human side is any less than my dragon side?" Millie asked.

Looking surprised, Audun backed up a step. "You're the one who has doubts. Lack of confidence is rarely a dragon trait. As far as I know, humans are the only creatures who are ever uncertain about their own abilities."

"I'm not uncertain!" said Millie. "It's just that my magic isn't very strong and that's what we need to take care of this plant."

"I'll tell you what we'll do," Audun told her. "You stay here, and I'll go look." He started down the path, glancing from one side to the other.

"I will not!" Millie said as she hurried to catch up. "I came here on my mother's behalf, so *I* have to take care of this. You're the one who should stand back and wait for me to look into it!"

"Look," said Audun, gesturing at a tree a few yards away. "Is that the tree they were talking about? It has red berries."

It was a pretty little tree that couldn't have been more than seven feet tall. Its leaves were nearly heart shaped, and the branches bore clusters of red berries.

"They look like raspberries," said Millie, reaching out to pick one.

Audun knocked her hand aside. "Don't touch it!"

20

"Moss said it wasn't poisonous."

"She said she didn't know if it was poisonous, but she still thought it was dangerous. There's the dead bird she was talking about."

"And there are three more dead birds over here," Millie said.

"I saw some plants once that had branches like arms. The plants could move around. I wonder if this tree can, too."

Millie shook her head. "It doesn't look like it."

A breeze sprang up, shivering the leaves of the trees around them. Audun slapped at his cheek. "Something just stung me!"

Millie took a step toward him. "Let me see," she said. A flurry of loose leaves broke free from the tree and fluttered through the air. One brushed against her upraised hand. Millie cried out as blinding pain tore through her. She stared at her hand in horror, stumbling back until she bumped into the solid trunk of an old oak.

"What happened?" Audun asked, his hand pressed to his cheek.

"I don't know," Millie gasped. The pain radiating up her arm was so intense that she could think of nothing else.

"It must have something to do with that tree. We have to change, Millie. Do it now!"

"It hurts so much!"

"The change might help. Please, you have to try!"

Millie's entire body vibrated from the pain. It was hard to concentrate, but she forced herself. The transformation seemed to take forever, but then her skin turned from the soft flesh of a human to tough dragon hide and the pain ended with surprising abruptness. Millie turned to face Audun, who was now a dragon as well.

"Are you all right?" he asked, his voice heavy with concern.

"I am. Are you?"

Audun nodded. "Look," he said, striding closer to the tree. "The entire thing is covered with fuzz—the berries, the leaves, the bark—everything."

"Like a peach?" asked Millie, joining him beside the tree. She arched her neck for a better look. Dragon eyesight is far better than human, and she could now see things that she couldn't before.

"Not at all," said Audun. "Peach fuzz is soft. This stuff is more like tiny needles."

Millie glanced down at her front foot. She could see her dragon hide forcing the needles out even as she watched. When they were fully expelled, she exhaled a puff of flame, melting them like molten glass. "I can see why the fairies were afraid of the tree."

"They should have told us what to expect," said Audun.

"Fairies rarely do what they should," said Millie. "They don't think about things the way we do."

22

A breath of air rustled the leaves again. This time Millie could see the cloud of tiny needles that swept from the tree into the surrounding forest.

"What do you want to do about the tree?" Audun asked.

"Burn it to the ground," Millie said, backing away. "The fairies were right. This tree is too dangerous and shouldn't be here."

Audun stood to the side while Millie blasted the tree with fire, letting her flame wash over it so that she burned the tiny needles as well as the plant itself. When she was finished and there was nothing but ash, Audun stepped forward and began digging up the ground where the tree had stood. "Remember those plants . . . I . . . told you about?" he asked, puffing with exertion. "I thought I'd killed them . . . but just a few weeks later . . . they started to grow again. If we really want to . . . get rid of this tree . . . we have to destroy . . . the roots as well."

"Good idea," said Millie.

A dragon's talons are tougher than metal yet refined enough to pluck a gnat from the air without hurting it. Millie watched as Audun dug up the roots, knowing that he would find every one. She waited until he was out of the way, then burned every scrap of root to ashes, too.

"That was awful!" Millie said as they returned to the spot where she'd left her magic carpet.

They flew back to the castle side by side. Millie was delighted with what she'd been able to accomplish, but she couldn't help wondering what she would have done if the task had required the kind of magic she didn't have.

Millie was relieved when she found her parents waiting for her in the Great Hall and couldn't wait to tell them what had happened. But before she could say a word, her mother kissed her on her human-again cheek and said, "Your father and I are leaving. Grassina and Haywood should have returned by now. I told your father I was worried, and he suggested that we go to the island to see if they need our help. I'm sure your father is right and nothing bad has happened, but I can't help thinking that we should have heard from them."

"And when we get there and your mother sees that everyone is fine, she and I might just take a few days to enjoy the beach," said Eadric, Millie's father. "We haven't been there in years."

"We shouldn't be gone long," said Emma. "Your grandparents will be in charge of any nonmagical issues, but I'm depending on you and your cousin, Francis, to help out if any magical problems come up. And keep an eye on Felix, too, if you would. His nursemaid has everything under control, but I'd feel better if I knew you were watching over him as well."

"Of course I'll keep an eye on Felix, but are you sure you have to go?" Millie asked, and immediately felt selfish and petty. This was her great-aunt and great-uncle her mother was talking about, people who were very dear to her. If they needed help, her parents had to go. But being left alone to deal with all of the magical problems . . . Francis would be there, but she couldn't imagine that he'd be much help. He was so preoccupied with becoming a knight that he never spent much time on his other magical studies, even though he was more gifted than Millie. If she had half the magic he had, she would have studied every book and parchment she could get her hands on . . .

"Don't you worry about a thing," Audun told her parents, pulling Millie to his side and giving her a reassuring hug. "I'll be here to help Millie and Francis if they need it. I'm sure there won't be any problems that the three of us can't handle."

Three

Two days later, Millie learned that something was harassing the residents of the tiny village of Dewly Glen. She hurried to her aunt's cottage to ask Francis to go with her, but he was sound asleep in bed.

"You'll have to go without me," he mumbled when she shook him awake. "I just got back from chasing will-of-the-wisps out of the swamp. It took me all night to get rid of them."

"But Francis," she said as he closed his eyes again, "you're the one with the magic!"

"You'll manage, I'm sure," he said, pulling the covers over his head.

Millie turned to Audun, who was waiting by the door. "I don't even know what I'm going to face. The man who left word was gone before I could talk to him."

"Don't look so worried," Audun said, taking her hand. "When I was little, my grandmother Song of the Glacier always told me, 'Dragons can do anything if it's worth doing.'"

"I didn't know it until recently, but apparently my grand-mother Frazzela used to say that the only good dragon is a dead dragon. That's one of the reasons we didn't see her very often."

"Huh," said Audun. "Song of the Glacier used to say the same thing about humans, which is probably why she hasn't warmed up to your family yet."

"You didn't tell me she hates humans! Maybe we shouldn't invite her to the wedding."

"I wouldn't go that far," said Audun. "I'm sure she won't do anything unpleasant, and there's no use worrying about something that probably won't happen. Like what-ever's bothering the people of Dewly Glen—you shouldn't worry about how you're going to handle it until you know what it is. It might not be much at all."

"I suppose," said Millie. "Or it could be something really nasty. Being dragons helped us last time, but that doesn't mean it always will. One of these days I'm going to run into a problem that fire and strength can't solve."

Audun shaded his eyes as they stepped outside into the bright sunlight. "Maybe, although it's hard to imagine what that might be. We should probably take your magic carpet again."

Millie nodded. "Especially since we'll have to talk to people this time."

Dewly Glen was on the far side of the enchanted for-est, nearly two hours by magic carpet from the castle. Millie and Audun spent the time holding hands and talking as the carpet skimmed just above the tops of the tallest trees.

"Do dragons have family names?" Millie asked.

"No, we don't. Our mothers give us our first names, then we choose our own adult names when we're old enough."

"How old is that?" asked Millie.

"That depends on the dragon," he replied. "It could be anywhere from twenty years to two hundred. My father didn't choose his until he was sixty-three. What's your family name?"

"Verderia. It's from my mother's side. In Greater Greensward, the crown goes to the eldest daughter, unless her parents declare her unfit or she marries and moves far away. That's happened only once, and they say that princess had never wanted the crown. Her younger sister became queen and was said to be a good one. All the women of Greater Greensward had only daughters for as long as anyone could remember, until Great-Aunt Grassina had Francis and Mother had Felix."

"Why would a girl be declared unfit for the crown?" Audun asked.

"Lots of reasons, but usually because she'd fallen victim to the curse that said that girls in our family would become nasty hags if they touched a flower after turning sixteen. Our family history would have been a lot different if that curse had never been cast. I'm so glad my mother was able to end it. If she hadn't, my parents would never have gotten married and I wouldn't exist."

"Then I'm glad she got rid of the curse, too. My life would be nothing without you in it." Audun leaned closer to kiss her and Millie turned halfway around to face him. When they looked up again, they were both smiling. "Go on," he said. "I think your family history is interesting."

Millie cleared her throat and said, "There isn't much else to tell. The daughters who inherit the crown take the name Verderia to show that the line is unbroken, unless they move to their husband's kingdom and take his name."

"What about your father's side?"

"The crown is always passed down through the sons in Upper Montevista. The old ruling line died out almost three hundred years ago, and my father's ancestor won the crown through combat. His family name is Highwall."

"Since I don't have a family name, I guess you would keep the name Verderia, or would you choose Highwall?" asked Audun.

"It would have to stay Verderia. I don't have the magic to be the Green Witch, but I'm still the oldest daughter so I'll probably be queen someday. Felix will be the next heir to the throne of Upper Montevista after Father."

"Verderia. I like the sound of that," Audun said, kissing her on the tip of her nose. "Now tell me, where exactly is Dewly Glen? We haven't passed it, have we?"

"Not yet," said Millie. "But we should be close."

Although Millie had flown over Greater Greensward as a dragon countless times and knew where every village was located, she had never actually visited Dewly Glen.

She preferred seeing villages for the first time with her mother, who, as the Green Witch, had made a point of visiting them all long before Millie was born. People knew her mother and were comfortable talking to her; no one in Dewly Glen knew Millie.

It was a small village on the edge of the forest only a few miles from Greater Greensward's eastern border and the kingdom of Soggy Molvinia. Tiny cottages with thatched roofs and walls of sticks and dried mud lined a narrow dirt road running through the center of the village and south past the ancient trees of the enchanted forest. Beyond the last of the cottages lay a scattering of small, cultivated fields where men and women tended the crops.

Millie landed her carpet in the middle of the main road amid a cloud of swirling dust. She and Audun stood up, coughing, and, when the dust cleared, were surprised to see an elderly couple watching them from under the eaves of a nearby cottage.

"Hello!" Millie wheezed as she tried to catch her breath.

"Huh," grunted the old man.

The old woman continued to bounce the infant she held in her arms without saying a word. A small child peeked through the doorway but didn't come out. Another young child began to wail inside the cottage. The old woman turned and went in. A moment later the wailing stopped, leaving only the strident chirring of insects.

"Where is everyone?" asked Audun.

The old man spat into the dust, then jerked his chin toward the small patches of farmland that lay beyond the village. "In the fields," he said.

Millie peered into the shadow under the eaves. The man's face was scratched, as were his neck and wrists. He had purple smudges under his eyes as if he hadn't gotten much sleep. "I'm Princess Millie and this is my betrothed, Audun," she said. "We're here on behalf of my mother, the Green Witch. I understand you've been plagued by some kind of beast. We've come to help you."

"We don't need your help," he said, wiping his chin and lower lip with the back of his hand.

Millie sighed. "Even so, I need to see what—"

A loud blast of discordant notes drowned out the sound of the insects. Both Millie and Audun looked around, startled, but the old man didn't seem surprised. Before they could ask him what had made the sound, the man hustled back into his cottage and closed the door.

"Now I'm really curious," said Millie. "Let's go find someone who's willing to talk to us."

They had taken only a few steps in the direction of the fields when a creature the size of a six-month-old kitten launched itself at Millie, digging its claws into her leg and trying to climb her like a tree. She thought it *was* a kitten until she saw its face. Although the creature was covered with a thin layer of gray fur, the face was shaped like a man's and had a man's nose, mouth, and eyes. Millie reached

31

down, trying to grab the little creature by the scruff of its neck, and it opened its mouth to bite her. She jerked her hand back when she saw that it had three rows of very sharp teeth.

"Get off me!" said Audun.

Millie looked up to see Audun shaking his leg, too, trying to dislodge a small, orange-striped beast. When the creature climbing her leg dug its claws in to go higher, she yelped, grabbed it, and pulled it away from her body. She examined the spitting, snarling creature and was surprised when it spoke to her in a man's voice. "Let me go, or I'll tear out your gizzard and eat it for my midday munchies!"

"You'll do no such thing," said Millie. "If I put you down, I expect you to behave yourself. And tell your friend to behave himself, too."

"What is this thing?" Audun asked. He raised his arm and held the orange creature upside down by the ball attached to the end of its tail, making the little creature yowl and thrash.

"Put me down!" it screamed, swiping at Audun with its claws extended. "How dare you treat me like this! Don't you know who I am?"

"You're a baby—"

"I'm no baby! My babies' babies are having babies! Put me down before I—"

"I think they might be manticores," said Millie. "Or at least they're descended from a manticore. Grassina told me that when she was young, she conjured up a manticore from a tooth my great-grandmother had given her. When the beast wouldn't go away, Grassina cast a spell and made it kitten-sized. It must have mated with a cat and these are its progeny. Do you suppose that someone in the field could tell us . . . Oh, they've all run off!"

The people who had been working in the field just minutes before had disappeared while Millie and Audun were occupied with the odd creatures. They had been in such a hurry that they left their tools on the ground behind them.

"Then we'll go talk to the old man," Audun said, his face looking grim. "I don't care if he wants to talk to us or not."

Still carrying the little creatures at arm's length, Millie and Audun returned to the cottage and knocked on the door. They could hear muted voices inside, but no one answered.

"If no one comes to talk to us, I think we should open the door and toss these little monsters in," Audun said in a loud voice. "One . . . two . . ."

The old man opened the door muttering to himself. A little boy about eight years old pushed past him to stare wide-eyed at Millie and Audun. He looked much like the old man must have when he was a boy.

"Is this what you didn't want to talk about?" asked Audun, holding up the wriggling ball of teeth and fur.

The old man flinched and placed a hand on the boy's shoulder, pulling him back a step.

Millie gave the man her sternest look. "Why didn't you send word to the castle that these creatures were harassing you? Don't deny they are, because I can see the scratches."

The old man coughed into his hand and seemed unable to meet their eyes. "It's kind of embarrassing-like. What were we supposed to say—we've got a plague of kittens drivin' us crazy? Every time we come outside, they pound on us with those balls on the end of their tails, an' rip into us with their claws. You can't walk under a tree without the little monsters landing on your head and bitin' at your ears. No one can get a wink of sleep, either, what with the racket they make soon as the sun goes down."

"What racket?" asked the creature dangling from Audun's hand.

The one that Millie still held twisted around in her grasp to face the old man. "Those are love songs!" it said, sounding indignant.

The old man eyed the little beasts warily. "They don't sound like love songs to me. They sound like a whole bunch of people blastin' away on broken trumpets."

"Tell 'em about the dogs, Grandpa," said the little boy.

The old man nodded. "We tried handlin' it ourselves—borrowed some top-notch huntin' dogs—but the darn cats drove 'em off and now we have to pay the hounds' owner. Good hounds don't come cheap, let me tell you! Those blasted kittens—"

"They're manticores, not kittens!" said Millie.

"Whatever you want to call 'em, the hounds ran off with their tails between their legs the first time the little monsters yowled. Then we tried trapping the . . . manticores . . . , but they were too smart for us. They sprang the traps, stole the bait, and left the traps in the road. We heard 'em laughin' at us when we came out in the morning."

"It was funny!" said the orange-striped manticore.

"How many are there?" asked Audun.

"I don't rightly know," the man replied. He rubbed his chin and added after a moment, "Couple dozen, I expect. They come out a few at a time during the day, but they all come out at night, leastwise it sounds that way."

"Then that's when we'll come back," said Millie. "One more question before we go. What do they eat?"

"Just about anything, I think. They ate all our chickens, and we haven't seen nary a mouse nor a rat since they got here."

"They ate all the frogs in the pond, too, Grandpa," said the little boy. "And I saw one eat a snake yesterday."

"They may be small, but they've got powerful appetites."

"It sounds like it," said Audun. "Do you have somewhere we can keep these two for now where they can't get away?"

"I have an empty barrel you can use if you'll put 'em in and take 'em out. But if you come back tonight, watch your step. Those little monsters like to trip you in the dark."

35

They were seated on the magic carpet flying over the enchanted forest once again when Millie asked, "You have a plan, don't you?"

Audun nodded. "We'll trap them, but our trap won't look like one. I caught a desicca bird by hiding in the sand once. With the right kind of bait, I should be able to catch some miniature manticores the same way. We just need to get a few things at that fishing village I saw on the river last week and we'll be all set."

It was dusk when they returned to the village of Dewly Glen. This time they arrived as dragons, flying so high over the forest that anyone looking up would see little dots and think they were birds. Even from high up, their dragon vision could make out the tiny figures in the village going about their business. Millie and Audun waited, gliding on updrafts until the last door was closed and the last window shuttered. Moving as silently as wind and wing allowed, they spiraled down, landing in a grove of trees.

They waited until they heard the voices of manticores coming from the village before creeping to a mound of dirt just beyond the last cottage. Keeping an eye out for the little beasts, Audun curled up in a circle and lay still while Millie covered his body with dirt. When only his face was exposed, Millie stepped to the center of the circle and set down a large wooden box made to trap fish. She opened the lid and a torrent of mice poured from the box. Before they could scurry off, Millie untied a cloth bag and took out a wheel of cheese, which she dropped on the ground beside the box. Their noses quivering, the mice turned to the wheel of cheese. With a beat of her wings, Millie rose into the air and returned to the trees, where she hunched down, waiting for Audun's signal.

Both dragons lay still, their ears pricked as they listened to the cacophony of the manticores' voices. Nearly half an hour passed before a manticore came close enough to smell the scent of the mice. Blaring the news of his discovery, the beast summoned his friends to the feast. Millie's limbs twitched as she readied herself to fly to Audun, but she didn't open her wings until he raised his head and coughed, a loud sharp sound that made mice and manticores freeze where they stood. Only a few heartbeats later she was landing beside Audun, who had shaken himself free of the dirt and was catching manticores and stuffing them into the wooden box through a small door on the side. The beasts became frantic when they discovered that the door didn't open outward and that they were trapped. The little creatures in the box filled the air with the ear-shattering din of their distress, while the ones outside fought with tooth and claw, neither of which could penetrate the dragons' hide. It took both dragons' efforts to collect the beasts and shove them into the box as they tried to escape.

When the last one was in the box and the door was securely fastened, Millie sat back with a sigh. "Remind me never to do that again. My great-grandmother shut wasps and bees in a crate once. I think this might have been worse."

"Wait, here's another one," Audun said, dragging a particularly stubborn manticore away from his tail, where it had been gnawing with much effort and no effect.

Millie opened the door so he could shove the little beast inside. The noise in the box was so loud it made even the dragons wince. "Do you think that was all of them?" she said, looking around.

Audun refastened the latch on the box. "I hope so, but there's no way of telling, at least not tonight."

"We'll have to come back in a few days and ask the villagers," said Millie.

"Let us outta here!" shouted a voice from inside the box.

"We will!" Millie shouted back. "As soon as we get where we're going."

"And that can't be any too soon," said Audun. He sniffed the air, his nostrils flaring. "We need to finish this and get back to the castle before dawn. I think a nasty storm is headed this way, and I don't want to get caught in it if we can help it."

When they took off, Millie carried her magic carpet in her claws while Audun lugged the box. The flight north was a familiar one, although neither of them had passed that way in more than a year. The two dragons flew side by side, soaring over grasslands, forests, and a few scattered

villages where only the sleepless would have seen the dragon silhouettes against the bright disk of the moon. They reached the mountains in the early hours of the morning, when the air was still and every sound seemed loud. Tall mountain peaks surrounded the valley where they landed and set down the crate. Although it was midsummer and there was grass under their feet, the air was chilly enough to turn to fog with each puff of Millie's breath. A stream ran through the center of the valley, its water nearly as cold as the ice from which it came, but the dragons bent down to taste it and found it pure and sweet.

Audun opened the crate, releasing the kitten-sized beasts. Once out of the crate, the manticores made such a clamor that the echo seemed to shake the mountains themselves, yet the beasts had no interest in either attacking or fleeing from the dragons. Instead they stood in a group, peering into the dark while the balls on the tips of their tails twitched in agitation.

"What is this place?" asked one as Millie and Audun prepared to leave.

"Somewhere that you can do anything you want without hurting anyone," said Millie.

"You should be fine here," Audun added. "There are caves where you can live when the snows get deep, and you'll find plenty of fish in the stream."

"And mice!" said a manticore just before it pounced on something small and furry rustling the grass.

"Good luck!" said Millie as she and Audun took to the air.

"They're going to need it if they try crossing those mountains," Audun told her. "Those peaks are higher than they look."

⤐

They were on their way back to Greater Greensward when Millie said, "I've been thinking. Why do you suppose no one saw the manticores until now? I mean, if they were descended from that one Grassina changed, why didn't they make their presence known before this? It's been years since Grassina was a girl and used her magic on that manticore."

"That's a good question," said Audun. "It does seem odd that they'd appear so suddenly."

Millie nodded. "Like that awful tree with the spines. All this *would* have to happen while my mother and Grassina were away!"

"Yes," Audun said, looking thoughtful. "It's almost as if someone had planned it that way."

⤐

The storm that Audun had predicted caught up with them as they were flying south over the Bullrush River. A gentle rain pattered on their backs for a few minutes before turning into a torrent. Water pelted their faces and sluiced down their scales, running into their eyes so that they had to close their second set of eyelids to see. Although the

lids were transparent, they made everything look a little less distinct. The wind grew fierce, pummeling them. Lightning flashed as the dragons flew over the enchanted forest, and they landed at the castle in a deluge that had already made the moat overflow its bank and created small rivers within the castle grounds. The sky was so heavy with thick, gray clouds that even if the sun were high, its light couldn't have gotten through.

Millie was convinced that it had to be past dawn when she and Audun landed in the courtyard and ran up the castle steps. They both changed back to their human forms as soon as they were inside, shuddering in the pounding rain that soaked them to the skin even as they worked together to close the door against the force of the wind.

Sighing with relief, Millie led the way to the Great Hall, a shortcut to the stairs that led to their rooms and dry clothes. Although Millie wasn't surprised to see the torches lit as if it were still night, she didn't expect to see a murmuring crowd gathered around her grandmother in the Hall. Queen Chartreuse was wringing her hands as tears streamed down her pale cheeks. Guards strode purposefully through the Hall, their expressions somber.

"Grandmother, what's wrong?" Millie asked, running to the side of the queen.

"Felix is gone!" sobbed Queen Chartreuse. "Someone came in the night and stole him away!"

Four

W hat do you mean, someone stole Felix?" asked Millie. "Are you sure, because one day last month I went to see him and he'd been fussy and his nursemaid had taken him for a walk. I was sure he'd been kidnapped until I found them in the garden."

A middle-aged woman standing behind the queen wailed and buried her face in her hands. Sobbing loudly, the woman ran from the Hall.

"What's wrong with her?" said Audun.

Millie frowned, staring at the door through which the figure had just disappeared. "That was his nursemaid. I guess that means she's not with him. Can someone please tell me what happened?"

A tall, distinguished-looking man with white hair and a trim white beard had just come into the Hall through a different door. "I can tell you," King Limelyn, her grandfather, said. "His nursemaid said she'd heard a strange sound in the corridor outside your brother's chamber. She went into the hallway to investigate and found nothing unusual. When she tried to go back into Felix's room, the door was locked. She ran down the corridor to call for the guards; the door was standing open when they arrived. They hurried in to investigate and found the baby's crib empty. I've had my men search every floor, but so far we haven't found even the smallest clue as to what might have happened."

"I knew your mother shouldn't go away!" the queen wailed. "Those old witches had no right to ask Grassina for help and she had no right to go. And then your mother went traipsing off after her! Both of my daughters are more interested in helping others than they are in seeing to their responsibilities here at home. If they had been here, none of this would have happened."

"That's not fair, Grandmother," said Millie. "My mother does what she feels she has to and so does Great-Aunt Grassina. They work hard for Greater Greensward and you know it."

"Your grandmother is just upset, Millie," said the king. "We're all very worried. If my men don't find your brother, we may need to ask for magical help."

"Audun and I can look, too," said Millie. "There has to be something that can tell us what happened to Felix."

Millie and Audun ran up the steps to the baby prince's room. Guards were inspecting the doorway and the corridor, but the room inside was empty. The prince's crib stood against the far wall, holding nothing more than a light silk blanket and a golden rattle shaped like a frog. "Poor Felix,"

Millie said with a catch in her voice as she touched the blanket with tentative fingers. "Whoever took him had better not hurt him. If they do, I'll hunt them down myself. This is my fault, you know. My mother asked me to look after Felix, and I let someone kidnap him!"

"You didn't *let* anyone do anything," said Audun, wrapping his arms around Millie and pulling her close. "Your mother also asked you to take care of the kingdom, which is what you were doing. And now we'll deal with this. We'll find your little brother before anything can happen to him."

"But what if something already has?" said Millie.

Audun's expression became cold and hard. "Then the monster who hurt that baby will have two dragons who won't stop until every last scrap of him is torn to shreds. But before we plan his demise, let's see what we can find. Our eyesight is better as dragons. Maybe we'll see something everyone else has missed."

Millie nodded. "Unless it was a ghost, he must have left some sign that he was here, and a ghost can't carry off a baby."

It took them only a moment to turn into dragons. The room had looked well scrubbed and spotless while they were human, but now Millie could see every speck of dust on the chair backs and the lid of the trunk, every smudge on the floor, and every piece of lint on the baby's bedding. Her hearing was better, too, and she could make out the distinct sound of each raindrop hitting the wall outside the window.

While Audun inspected the area around the door, Millie moved toward the window, casting back and forth, with her nose inches from the stone surface. "Look here," she finally said, pointing to a spot just under the window ledge. "There's dirt on the floor here that I haven't seen anywhere else in the room."

"Let me see," Audun said, lumbering toward her.

"What do you think?" Millie asked as Audun sniffed the dirt.

Using his talon, he poked the little clump until it fell apart. "Looks like dirt to me."

Millie sighed and sat back on her haunches. "I don't know what to do, Audun. If my mother were here, she could say a spell and have the walls tell us what happened."

Audun laughed. "From what I know about the Green Witch, she could have the dirt talk to us and tell us where it came from. You should hear what the dragons back on King's Isle say about her!"

"I wish she were here," said Millie. "Grandmother was right, in a way. This probably wouldn't have happened if Mother had been home."

The rain that had been pouring so fiercely just minutes before had begun to slack off. Millie was looking out the window at the now-brightening sky when she heard the faintest of sounds. *Scritch! Scritch!* She turned around, bumping into Audun as he too turned to see what was making the sound. *Scritch! Scritch!* The sound came again.

"It's coming from the trunk," said Millie. "Maybe it's a mouse."

Something thumped in the trunk. "It would have to be an awfully big mouse," said Audun. He lifted the lid and jerked his head back in surprise. "Millie, I think this might be a friend of yours."

Millie peered into the trunk and gasped. Two small bats lay on top of the folded baby clothes. "Zoë!" Millie exclaimed. "Li'l! Who did this to you? Are you all right?" Her two friends were struggling to sit up when Millie reached into the trunk and lifted them out.

"I could hardly breathe in there!" said Zoë.

"Did you find your brother yet?" Li'l asked, her eyes frantic.

The air shimmered around Zoë as she changed back into her human form. Her mother, Li'l, had married Garrid, a vampire, which was why her children could become human.

"What do you know about Felix?" said Millie. "Did you see whoever took him?"

Zoë shook her head. She picked up her mother and carried her to the nearest bench. When Li'l fluttered to her daughter's shoulder, Zoë sat down with a sigh and said, "We didn't see much of anything."

Li'l stretched her cramped wings, groaning softly. "That's true. We were out catching bugs when we saw a strange light coming from that window," she said, pointing with a wingtip at the only window in the room. "We flew in to investigate and a blast of air hit us."

"It felt like a giant had slapped us to the ground," said Zoë.

"When we came to, we were in the trunk—"

"Like old clothes," Zoë added.

"And we couldn't get out."

"We could hear everything, though," said Zoë. "We heard the guards talking about how Felix was missing. We both shouted, but I guess the rain was so loud that no one could hear us."

"Whoever took your brother must have already been gone by the time we woke up," said Li'l.

"So we're no closer to knowing who took him," Millie said.

"Yes, we are," replied Audun. "Whoever took him must have used magic to do it, which was more than we knew a minute ago. We should go tell your grandfather so he doesn't waste his time searching the castle."

"And *we* should go home," Li'l told her daughter. "Your father probably won't be able to get a wink of sleep until he knows that we're all right, and he should have gone to bed hours ago."

Zoë stood and turned to Millie. "Let us know if there's anything we can do."

"We will," Millie promised.

A moment later Zoë was a bat again and she and her mother were flying out the window.

47

Millie and Audun went to the Great Hall, but it was nearly deserted. They learned from a passing guard that the queen had retired to her chamber and the king had gone into the dungeon.

"Do you suppose he went to consult with the ghosts?" Audun asked Millie as they descended the dungeon steps.

Millie shook her head. "Neither of my grandparents likes talking to the ghosts. My grandmother still tries to pretend they don't exist. Grandfather isn't quite so bad, but he avoids them whenever possible. I don't think it would occur to him to ask a ghost for help or advice. No, I'm sure he's down here for another reason."

The dungeon felt especially damp after the downpour. Millie knew the dungeon as well as she did the upper floors of the castle and could find anything, even when errant magic had relocated the doors or opened holes in the floors. There wasn't as much wild magic running loose in the dungeon as there had been when her mother was young, but it still showed up now and then. Because of the bottomless pits that appeared occasionally, it was never wise to run through the dungeon, no matter what was chasing you; when the air suddenly turned cold and an aged ghost came toward them, Millie told Audun not to move.

The ghost ran down the corridor, shrieking with rage at Millie and Audun. His long hair streamed behind him, and his ragged tunic flapped around the vague shape of his emaciated body. "Come to steal my medallion, have you?"

he screamed, brandishing a ghostly pike. "I'll show you what happens to thieves!"

Audun gasped as the ghost ran him through with the pike. The dragon looked down in horror, then glanced up in confusion when he realized that he hadn't felt a thing.

"He can't hurt you," Millie told him. "Most ghosts can't do more than frighten you into doing something foolish, in which case you might hurt yourself. Hubert," she said, turning to the ghost, "why do you think we want to steal your medallion?"

"Because there's a thief in the castle and it might be you!"

A tall, elegant-looking ghost dressed in a peaked cap and overtunic glided down the corridor to float between Hubert and the princess. "Hubert thinks that because someone took your little brother, they want to steal the valuables, too. If anyone is going to steal your medallion, Hubert," he said, turning to the first ghost, "it would be the hamsters. If you're so worried about your medallion, go watch over it and stop bothering the princess," he said, making shooing motions with his hands.

Grumbling to himself, Hubert disappeared through a wall.

"Thank you, Sir Jarvis," said Millie. "I didn't know that Hubert was so worried about his medallion."

The noble ghost sighed. "It was his most prized possession. The first princess Millie, the one you were named after, gave it to him for bravery. Just a few years before you were born, your family had the bones in the oubliette buried, but Hubert insisted the medallion stay here in the castle. Your mother hid the medallion in a special place. Though Hubert forgets everything else, he never forgets where that special place is located."

"So you've heard about Felix," said Millie. "Does anyone down here know who might have taken him?"

Sir Jarvis shook his head. "No one has been aboveground in days. Your great-grandparents are away at a meeting of the council of ghosts. We know only what we've heard people talking about when they visit the dungeon. Your grandfather passed through just a short time ago on his way to the secret passage. He was talking to his guards about your brother. They said—"

A roar so high pitched that it reached the very limit of what a human can hear echoed throughout the dungeon. Audun whipped his head around, and even Millie, who had heard it before, felt her heart leap in her chest. "That's the shadow beast," she said, taking a step toward Audun.

The air that had been cold before turned frigid as unseen figures rustled by them. Audun pulled Millie to his side when it sounded as if a crowd were passing them in the corridor.

"Everyone is headed toward the shadow beast. I'd better go help them," said Sir Jarvis. "We've been trying to capture the beast for the last few days. All of us other ghosts stand watch over the secret passage and warn the guards when the wall between the dungeon and the moat springs a leak. We think it's about time the shadow beast contributed, too, instead of just scaring our visitors."

As Sir Jarvis floated away, Millie and Audun began walking toward the end of the dungeon where the secret passage was located. "You haven't seen the shadow beast yet," said Millie. "No one knows what it was originally, because all you can see of the beast are its eyes and a shadow. It's a ghost, too, but the odd thing about it is that you can touch it, although only Grassina and my mother actually have. And if we can touch the beast, it can touch us, so everyone is afraid of it. The beast has never bothered me, but I've heard that it almost got my grandmother when she was young."

The roar rang out again, louder this time, as if the beast were coming closer. Millie glanced down the corridor and saw a shadow pass beneath the flickering light of the torches on the walls. "It's here!" she whispered, reaching for Audun's hand.

Audun took a single step forward. "Where?" he murmured. And then reddened eyes appeared in the shadow as the beast loped down the corridor.

"Watch out!" shouted Millie, but the beast was already on them.

It knocked Audun to the side with one powerful blow. He staggered and fell against the wall. It wasn't until the beast's eyes turned to Millie, however, that Audun's expression hardened and he began to change into a dragon. The change wasn't complete when the beast launched itself at

Millie, but Audun didn't wait—he threw himself between them even as his skin hardened into scales and his nails into talons.

Aside from its eyes, the beast looked like little more than a deepening of the shadows. It was hard to fight something he couldn't really see, but Audun managed somehow. Whipping his tail, he hit something with a good, hard *thwack*. A powerful swipe of his talons elicited another high-pitched roar. The beast leaped onto Audun's back, forcing him to the ground, but Audun shook off the weight and turned to face the shadow again. Another swing of his tail and the beast hit the wall hard enough to crack stone. The red eyes blinked, then moved from side to side as if a great beast were shaking its head.

"There it is!" shouted Sir Jarvis, appearing in the darkened corridor as a pale blue glow.

The beast backed away, its eyes watching the advancing ghosts as one blue glow after another joined Sir Jarvis. The ghosts began to take shape, becoming a little less transparent, although Millie could still see the walls of the dungeon through them. More appeared, coming through closed doors and solid stone walls. One materialized right in front of Millie. "Pardon me, Your Highness," he said, tipping his dented metal helmet.

Soon more than a dozen ghosts were crowding the shadow beast, and it began to pace as if looking for a way out. When the ghosts moved closer, the beast leaped, soaring over Audun and Millie and disappearing in the shadows behind them.

A shout went up from the ghosts and they gave chase, turning back by twos and threes into pale blue wisps that poured down the corridor after the shadow beast.

"You were amazing," Millie said, standing on tiptoe to kiss the dragon on the cheek.

"I wish I could exhale ice like Frostybreath can. That might have slowed the beast down," Audun said, turning back into his human form.

"Or done nothing at all," said Millie. "The shadow beast is a ghost, after all."

They found the king on the other side of the secret passage door talking to Millie's cousin, Francis. The king looked up as the door creaked open. "Any news?" he asked, sounding hopeful.

"No news of Felix, but we did learn something about the person who took him," said Millie. "He—or she—is a magic user." She continued by telling him what had happened to Li'l and Zoë.

King Limelyn didn't look happy. "I was afraid of that. If someone used magic to whisk Felix away, he or she could be anywhere by now. Francis and I have been inspecting the secret passage to make sure the kidnapper didn't go this way."

"We haven't found anything here, but then we wouldn't have if the kidnapper used magic or went out the window," said Francis. "I'm sorry I'm not more help. I've been focusing my study of magic on ways to make myself a better knight. I should have listened to my parents and broadened my studies to include a wider range of magic. I can't do much unless I can see my enemy."

"If we need magic to help us find magic," Millie said, "we'll have to go ask someone who can do the right kind of spells. I'm going to the enchanted forest to see if any of the three witches are home."

Five

The cottage lay in the heart of the enchanted forest, far from any other human or witch dwelling. It had once belonged to a would-be witch who had captured Millie's mother after Emma had been turned into a frog, but now it was the home of three real witches, two of whom were sisters. Although all three witches were friends of her family, Millie was especially fond of Azuria, the Blue Witch, and it was Azuria whom Millie and Audun first saw when they landed in the field beside the cottage.

"Hello, Millie! Hello, Audun!" the witch shouted as she ran past, waving a butterfly net. A sapphire blue butterfly zigzagged just out of reach as the elderly woman lunged after it, her net snapping in the air.

The air around them shimmered as the two dragons turned into their human form and stood waiting for Azuria to come back. When the old witch continued to dart around the field, Millie looked at Audun and shrugged. "Maybe we should talk to someone else."

They could hear voices arguing inside the cottage as they drew closer, so they knew that the two sisters were home. Millie's mouth watered at the scent of fresh-baked cherry pie, and she smiled when Audun raised his nose to sniff. She knocked on the door, and a moment later it opened with a bang. A woman with gray hair and bright blue eyes greeted them, reaching out a flour-covered hand to gesture them inside. Her name was Oculura and she carried a large wooden batter-filled bowl. She was stirring her wooden spoon with so much energy that the batter sloshed over the sides, splattering her clothes, the walls, and the floor. "Come in, come in and make yourselves comfortable," said Oculura. "Dyspepsia, clear off that bench so our guests can sit down."

"Don't you tell me what to do!" said an even older white-haired woman as she swept a pile of clean clothes off the bench and into her arms. Scowling at her sister, she stomped across the room and kicked the wall. The fireplace slid back, making a grinding sound and revealing another room beyond it.

"But that's an outside wall," Audun murmured into Millie's ear. "That's not possible."

The room they were standing in seemed bigger than she remembered it, and she thought the way the fireplace moved was definitely new. "They're witches," whispered Millie. "Anything is possible for them, which is why we came." In a louder voice, she said to Dyspepsia, "We need to talk to you."

"I'm busy," said the old woman. "Talk to Miss Bossy over there." Grumbling to herself, Dyspepsia flung the clothes through the doorway and kicked the wall again. "I'll deal with them later," she said as the fireplace swung back. Millie had to jump out of the way when the witch grabbed a broom and began to beat the floor with it, sending up thick clouds of dust.

"We need your help," Millie said, crossing the room to where Oculura was dumping batter into a pan.

"Dyspepsia, mind that dust!" shouted Oculura. "If you keep that up, there will be more dust than flour in this cake!"

"That would be an improvement," Dyspepsia replied.

"I can't talk to you now," Oculura told Millie. She scuttled across the room, moving a pan of cooling tarts from a table to the windowsill. "We couldn't sleep last night, what with that storm booming and banging, so I tried something new and made us all cups of sleep-tight tea. It worked very well because we slept like logs—"

"We slept like the dead," said Dyspepsia. "The house could have collapsed around our ears and we wouldn't have noticed. I told her this morning that that wasn't a good thing, but does she ever listen to me?"

"There's only one problem with sleep-tight tea," Oculura continued. "When you finally do wake up—"

"We slept hours past our usual get-up time," declared Dyspepsia, emphasizing each word with a *thwack* of the broom at whatever object was closest. Audun hopped out of the way when she turned in his direction.

57

"When you finally do wake up," Oculura repeated, "you have so much energy that you can't sit still. Azuria went outside to catch blue butterflies for a potion she invented, and I decided to cook. Dyspepsia said she's going to clean, but all she's done is make a bigger mess than before."

"That's not true!" snapped her sister. "This place hasn't looked this good in years!"

"The extra energy isn't supposed to last long," said Oculura. "No more than an hour or two."

"Don't listen to her. It's been two hours and forty-seven minutes since I woke up." Dyspepsia jabbed the broom at an hourglass filled with sand, knocking it onto the floor so that it shattered, spilling sand across Millie's shoes.

Oculura began to crack eggs into a bowl. "Normally, I'd use magic for this, but I have to use all this energy somehow. You'll have to stay for supper. I've already made too much food for just the three of us."

"Actually," said Millie as she tried to get out of Dyspepsia's way when the old woman began to attack the spilled sand with a broom. "We're in a hurry, so—"

The door behind her creaked open and Azuria shuffled in carrying a woven basket with a wooden lid. She dragged her feet as she crossed the room and collapsed onto the bench, dropping the basket on the floor beside her. "Every muscle in my body hurts," she said, slumping against the wall. "My bones, too. I'm too old for this."

"See," said Oculura, "she's used up her extra energy."

Azuria shook her head. "That wasn't *extra* energy. I've used up every bit of energy I would have had this week and next. I don't think I'll be able to move again until spring."

"I'm still going strong," Dyspepsia announced. "When I finish sweeping, I'm going to . . ." She took a step and staggered. Reaching out her hand, she grabbed hold of the edge of the table for support. "I guess that's it for me. The end sure does come fast."

"I don't understand," said Oculura. "You both drank more tea than I did, but I still have loads of energy. Who would like a nice plate of . . . Oh, I see what you mean. It sort of hits you all of a sudden." Putting her hand to her head, she swayed on her feet until Millie helped her to a seat beside Azuria.

"Don't ever make that tea again," said Dyspepsia. "I haven't been this tired since those villagers chased me out of town back when I was young and spry."

Oculura nodded. "Sounds good to me. But at least we got a lot accomplished."

"And I got a good night's sleep," Dyspepsia admitted. "That's pretty rare these days."

So," Oculura said, glancing at Millie, "what was it you wanted to see us about?"

"Felix is gone," Millie said. "Someone kidnapped him during the storm."

The three witches looked shocked. "Oh no!" Azuria gasped. "That sweet little baby!"

"Who would do such a thing?" demanded Oculura.

"A no-good scoundrel who should be tied in a sack and tossed in a river," Dyspepsia said. "That's what I wanted to do to the last man who jilted me. I might still have the sack, if you want me to look for it."

"First things first, Dyspepsia," said Azuria. "We have to find dear little Felix and catch the horrid scoundrel before we can use your sack. Now, what can you tell us about the kidnapping?" she asked, turning to Millie.

"Audun and I were gone when it happened. We were taking care of a problem with manticores, and when we got home we learned that someone had distracted Felix's nursemaid and taken him from his crib. Zoë and Li'l said they saw a strange light in the baby's room and that a blast of air knocked them unconscious when they stopped to look. Mother and Great-Aunt Grassina are away, and so is my great-grandmother. Francis doesn't have the right kind of magic, so we are hoping you can help us find Felix."

"Of course we'll help!" said Oculura. "You're practically family! Would you mind getting my jar of eyeballs off that shelf? I'm too tired to move right now."

Millie ran to get the jar and set it on the table in front of Oculura. After taking a pair of milky white eyes from the jar, the old woman bent over the table and popped out her bright blue ones. With the new eyes in her sockets, she stared off into space, seemingly looking at nothing.

"Those are her seer's eyes," Dyspepsia whispered to Audun. "She can use them to see into the future or the past. They aren't pretty, but they get the job done."

Oculura sighed and reached for the jar. "Except for now. They aren't working. All I can see are clouds and rain. That storm seems to have blocked everything."

"Fetch me my scrying bowl, Millie," said Dyspepsia. "It's the shiny silver bowl on the top shelf. That's it. Now bring it here. Oh, and get me a dipper of water; I don't need much. Now step back and let me look." The elderly witch passed her wrinkled hand over the bowl, then leaned forward until it looked as though she was about to dip her face in it. Millie couldn't see what she was looking at, but it wasn't long before Dyspepsia sat back with a grunt. "It's as Oculura said—all I can see are rain and clouds."

Azuria fumbled at the neck of her tunic. "We're not finished yet. I've had this farseeing ball for fifty-two years and it's never failed me." Pulling out a golden chain, she showed Millie a small crystalline ball held in place with a clasp shaped like a pair of tiny blue hands. Holding the ball up so everyone could see it, she murmured something and breathed onto the clear surface. Nothing happened for a moment, and Millie was sure it wasn't going to work, but then an image began to form. She leaned forward for a better look. The image was blurry, and Millie was willing it to become clearer when the farseeing ball suddenly filled with clouds. Azuria frowned and shook the ball. Rain slashed through it, seeming to splash and run down the ball's inner surface.

"Drat," said Azuria. "That's never happened before." She sighed and replaced the ball under the fabric of her tunic. "You know what it means if none of us can see what happened, don't you, ladies?"

Oculura nodded. "That storm wasn't natural. Whoever took the baby created that storm to block anyone from seeing what he was doing."

"Or she," said Dyspepsia. "I know a few witches who could have done this."

"We need to call for help." Azuria grunted as she reached down to her wicker basket and took out one of the blue butterflies. Holding it carefully between her cupped hands, she whispered to the insect, then opened her hands and set it free. The butterfly fluttered around her head before flying to the window and out into the sunlight. "I laid a compulsion on that butterfly," said the old woman. "She has to go find the fairy Moth and ask her to come here. Moth goes out at night. She might have seen that strange light you mentioned. If she did, it would have drawn her like, well, like a moth to flames." Azuria chuckled to herself as she sat back on the bench.

"Do you mean she might be able to tell us who took Felix?" asked Audun.

Azuria nodded. "I hope so."

"While we're waiting," said Oculura, "would anyone like a fruit tart or a slice of pie?"

"No thanks," Dyspepsia replied, making a face. "Watching you cook has put me off food."

Oculura had put vivid green eyes in her sockets. They seemed to get darker when she glared at her sister and said, "I thought you liked my cooking!"

While the two sisters argued, Millie joined Audun by the window. The sky had cleared and the rain had washed away the dust, leaving everything looking fresh and clean. Droplets sparkled in the sunlight, but Millie soon noticed that one sparkle seemed bigger than the rest and was moving toward them. It drew closer until she could make out the tiny figure of a fairy.

Millie and Audun stepped back when the fairy flew through the window and landed on the floor. In an instant, she turned from a fairy no bigger than half of Millie's little finger to one who was human sized. Her soft white wings and pale blue hair were very pretty, but Millie thought it was her large, dark eyes that made her look unusual. She seemed shy at first and uncomfortable at the scrutiny of so many people.

"Moth, I'd like you to meet our good friends Millie and Audun. Millie's mother is Princess Emeralda, the Green Witch."

Moth smiled and visibly relaxed. "I know your mother, Millie. She's a good friend to fairykind. From what I've heard, you are as well. Thank you for helping my friends Trillium, Moss, and Poison Ivy. If there's ever anything I can do for you . . ."

"Actually, we need your help right now," said Millie. "My mother is away and someone stole my baby brother during the night. We're trying to find out who took him."

"Did they leave another baby in his place?" the fairy asked.

Millie shook her head. "His crib was empty."

"Then it wasn't a fairy who took him. We always leave changelings to take the place of human babies."

Both Audun and Millie looked surprised, but the witches just nodded as if they'd heard it before. "You really do that?" said Millie. "I thought it was just a rumor."

"I never have, but I know other fairies who've done it. Human babies can be so cute!" said Moth.

Azuria cleared her throat. "What we really wanted to ask you was if you happened to notice a strange light coming from the castle last night. If you did, did you go to see what it was?"

Moth shook her head. "The storm was so awful that I spent the night in a hollow tree. I couldn't have flown in that wind if I'd wanted to, not without being blown halfway to the next kingdom. If I were you, I'd ask Raindrop. She learns a lot from listening to the falling rain."

"Of course!" said Azuria. "Why didn't I think of that? Thank you so much, Moth."

"I'm glad I could help," Moth said, shrinking once again. "We fairies do what we can!"

Six

The three witches were still debating how to contact Raindrop when Moth reappeared with Raindrop beside her. "I told Raindrop what you needed to know, so she insisted we go to the castle before coming here," Moth told them.

Raindrop nodded, her pale blue hair swirling around her delicate, pointy-chinned face. "Some people think I hear what the rain says only when it's falling, but I can hear it anytime, even after it's collected in a puddle!" She crinkled her nose and squinted when she glanced at Moth, as if to say that her friend was just such a person. "I wanted to listen to the raindrops where they collected in the puddles at the castle," she said, turning back to Millie. "I didn't know which window you meant, but I listened to each puddle till one mentioned a bright light. It told me that a person wearing a cloak came out through the high turret's window when the storm was at its worst. The figure was carrying a bundle, which could have been a baby, and flew off on a broom. I suppose the person was a witch. She went northeast, if you're interested."

"We're very interested," said Audun. "We have to find Felix and bring him back."

"I can go with you, if you want me to," Raindrop added. "The puddles will tell me where he went, but only for a little while. Once the rain dries up or gets soaked into the ground, it can no longer talk to me."

Millie felt as if a great weight had been lifted from her. She'd been so frightened that they'd never find her brother, but if the fairy could help find him . . .

"We're going, too," said Dyspepsia. "I wouldn't miss this for anything. We haven't had this much excitement around here since a boy griffin thought Oculura was a girl griffin and tried to carry her off."

"I was in the garden," said Oculura. "I don't know what he saw, but he sure liked it."

Dyspepsia chortled. "Maybe it was your feathered underwear."

"I didn't have any choice," said Oculura. "It was laundry day."

"We'll fly on our brooms, of course. I suppose you and Audun will travel by your usual method?" Dyspepsia asked.

Millie shrugged. "We have to. We didn't bring my magic carpet."

"What method is that?" asked Raindrop, quirking a pale blue eyebrow.

66

Audun and Millie smiled at each other as they stepped across the threshold and into the sunshine. "As dragons," Millie said as the air around them began to shimmer. She blinked as her eyes turned into those of a dragon. Colors looked different, and she could see the fairies even more clearly than before. Raindrop's blue hair had streaks of ultraviolet, a color Millie hadn't been able to see as a human.

Once everyone was outside, Moth decided that she wanted to go with them. "It looks like a party," she said, turning into her smaller self. "I can't resist a good party."

"It may take a while before I find more rain that can tell us anything," said Raindrop.

Moth zigzagged around her. "Then you'd best get started."

Millie, Audun, and the witches flew above the forest, circling while Raindrop looked for puddles. It took some time before she found one that could tell her about the cloaked figure. The tiny puddle was located in the crook of a tree and was nearly invisible to anyone in the air except a dragon or a fairy. The witches joined the two dragons to watch Raindrop scoop out a handful of water and bend down to listen as it dribbled back into the puddle. She looked satisfied when she glanced up to say, "The figure flew over this tree still headed northeast."

They moved more quickly after that, finding puddles in depressions in boulders, on top of witches' cottages, and in muddy dips in dirt roads. Moth finally grew tired of waiting for her friend and flew off, claiming that she was bored. The others followed Raindrop, anxiously awaiting her announcements each time she found the next puddle.

"Rain talks to all of us," she told them. "You just have to know how to listen."

They had left the forest behind when Azuria angled her broom so that she was flying next to Millie. "That's Soggy Molvinia," she said, pointing at the ground. "Most of the kingdom looks just like that."

Millie maintained the steady beat of her wings as she glanced down. Marshland stretched out in front of them for as far as she could see, making a crazy quilt of water and soggy patches of land. The bright colors of marsh flowers accented the mix of blues, browns, and greens like dabs of paint on an artist's palette.

Once again Raindrop flew down to listen to a shrinking puddle. She stayed on the ground for only a minute before darting back up to talk to Millie. "This is as far as I can go," she said. "The witch landed her broom on that hummock just as the rain stopped. She may have stayed here, or she may have gone on. Either way, I can't tell you what happened next. Falling rain notices everything, but puddles aren't very observant."

"Thank you so much," said Millie. "You've been such a big help."

"Just remember that," said Raindrop, "in case I need a favor someday." Bringing her hand to her lips, the fairy blew a kiss at Millie before darting back the way they had come.

"Now what?" asked Audun as the three witches gathered around them. "We can fly down there and look around, but that's an awful lot of ground to cover."

"I don't think we have much choice," Millie replied.

"I'm going to start by that hummock," said Azuria.

"We should all start there and work our way out," Audun said. "Millie and I will look from the air while you three ladies search the ground. If there's anything to find, we should be able to spot it with five of us looking."

"Oh dear," said Oculura. "I should have worn my blue eyes. These are fairly nearsighted, I'm afraid. I don't know how much help I'm going to be."

"And my back is hurting me," Dyspepsia whined. "I just can't ride a broom for long distances like I used to."

Azuria sighed. "Do what you can, girls. A child's life is at stake here."

"Yes, of course . . . ," said Oculura.

"I didn't mean . . . ," Dyspepsia protested even as Millie began to spiral closer to the ground.

While the three witches descended to the hummock, Millie and Audun began to search from the air. They didn't see much at first, but after a time Millie noticed a brown hummock much like the one where they'd left the witches. There was something odd about it, however, so she called to Audun and pointed at the little hill. "What does that look like to you?" she asked when Audun flew close enough to hear her.

"I don't know," Audun replied, squinting. "It almost looks like fabric, doesn't it? Let's get a better look."

The lower they went, the more puzzled Millie grew. It wasn't until the two dragons were about to touch the ground that she saw the brown mound for what it really was—a hunched figure wearing a cloak with the hood pulled up.

"It's the witch!" she breathed, but Audun had seen it as well, and he looked as if he was about to attack it. "No," said Millie. "You might hurt Felix."

Audun paused, his tail raised for a blow. He set it down reluctantly and, prepared to pounce, approached the seated figure.

"What took you so long?" asked the figure as he pushed back his hood. "I've been expecting you for hours."

Millie hissed as her breath escaped in a rush. It wasn't a witch at all. It was Olebald, the nasty old wizard. "Where's my brother? Do you have him with you?"

The old wizard shook his head and sneered. "I've put him where you'll never find him."

With a roar, Audun launched himself at Olebald and knocked him flat on his back. "What have you done with the baby?" the dragon growled.

When Olebald laughed, Audun pressed his talons against the old man's chest. Sweat broke out on the wizard's forehead and he gasped. "If you hurt me, that boy will spend the rest of his life in this marsh!"

"Where is he?" demanded Millie.

"Make Scaly Face get off me and I'll tell you."

The witches had noticed the commotion and flown closer to watch. Millie glanced up at them and saw Dyspepsia's mouth open in surprise. "Olebald, what are you doing here?" cried the old witch. "We were engaged to be married once," she told Millie.

"For about fifteen minutes!" said Olebald.

"Then he ditched me for a tree nymph!"

"And she tried to stuff me in a sack and throw me in the river!"

"It's too bad I didn't. Letting you talk me out of it was one of the dumbest mistakes I've ever made."

"That's saying a lot, considering how many dumb mistakes she's made," said her sister, Oculura.

Olebald's face was turning red when he shouted at Audun, "Let me go or I won't tell you a thing!"

Millie turned to Audun and nodded. Growling softly, the ice dragon sat back, freeing Olebald. The old man scrambled to his feet and straightened his cloak, revealing the broom he'd hidden under it. Snatching the knobbed wooden stick off the ground, he snickered and said, "You'll never find that baby. I turned him into a frog, and even I couldn't find him now. Do you know how many frogs there are in this marsh? Poor little princess," Olebald added, pretending to look sad. "Your brother is gone and so are your parents. You'll never see any of them again!"

Millie flinched as if she'd been struck. This time she didn't want to hold Audun back when he lunged for the wizard, but the old man was faster than anyone could have expected. Laughing triumphantly, Olebald smacked his broom against the ground . . . and vanished.

Dyspepsia squawked and nearly fell off her broom.

"Did you see that?" cried Oculura.

Azuria landed beside the two dragons, who were still staring at where Olebald had stood just a moment before. "He had it all planned, didn't he?" she said, using her toe to poke at a bristle that had fallen out of Olebald's broom. "He must have, to disappear like that. Olebald isn't a strong enough wizard to just vanish. He must have had a spell in place before we ever got here. All he had to do was tap the ground to put it into effect." She bent down to pick up a clump of dirt and crumbled it between her fingers. "If I'd had any inkling he was going to do it, I could have grabbed hold and followed him to wherever he went, but it's too late now. It was a one-shot spell. Ah well, live and learn. So, what did he tell you exactly?"

"He turned Felix into a frog," Audun said. "He set him loose in the marsh with all the other frogs."

"Oh dear," said Oculura.

"That's horrible," Dyspepsia declared.

"He said I'll never see Felix or my parents again," Millie said, sounding nearly as numb as she felt.

"You'll be able to find him, won't you?" Audun asked Azuria.

The Blue Witch shook her head. "It would take me weeks to find him among all the frogs here, and that's if he

72

doesn't swim farther away or get eaten. There are a lot of creatures in a marsh who consider frogs a delicacy."

Millie's face drained of color and she made a strangled sound. Her eyes looked stricken when she turned to Audun and said, "We have to find him soon!"

"Then we'll need your mother," said Azuria. "She's the most powerful witch I know."

"But I don't know how to get in touch with her," said Millie.

"You'll have to go get her. Do you know where she is?"

"She's on that tropical island where all the old witches were taken, but I don't know where the island is located."

"That's easy," said Azuria. "I've never been there myself, but I've heard that it's just past a string of islands that shoot melted rock into the sky."

Dyspepsia shook her head. "No it's not. It's all by itself halfway around the world, thousands of miles from anything."

"I was told that it was just off the coast of Grance," said Oculura. "They say the island is shaped like a rabbit with three ears and—"

"Never mind," said Millie. "I'm sure I'll find the way."

"You should go now, dear," said Oculura. "We'll stay here and look for Felix. Perhaps we'll be lucky and he'll come if we call him."

"Dragons know their names when they're babies, but do humans?" Audun asked.

Dyspepsia snorted. "I doubt it. But don't worry, we'll make sure nothing eats any of these frogs. Hey you, what do you think you're looking at? Shoo!" she shouted at a passing crow.

Millie thanked the witches, and a moment later she and Audun were airborne.

"It's good of them to help," said Audun. "Don't worry," he added when he saw Millie's expression. "Your mother will find him as soon as she gets back."

"That's another problem," said Millie, the creases in her brow deepening. "I still have no idea how to find the island."

Seven

$\mathcal{I}$t was late afternoon when Millie and Audun returned to Greater Greensward. They flew to the cottage where Francis lived with his parents, but he wasn't there so they continued on to the castle. Even from a distance Millie could see her cousin pacing the length of the curtain wall. He was wearing his armor as if expecting someone to attack the castle at any moment, and the polished metal reflected sunlight so that it hurt her eyes and she had to close her second set of lids.

"Any luck?" he called as she and Audun landed on the parapets.

Millie shook her head. "We know where Felix is, but we can't find him."

Francis looked puzzled. "That doesn't make any sense."

Agitated, Audun opened and closed his wings, making a sharp snapping sound each time. "It was Olebald Wizard who took him. I should have done something more permanent to him when we captured him in Aridia after the war over the throne. King Cadmus was sure he could keep him locked up, but Olebald is slippery and can escape from just about anything. He's been imprisoned in the dragon stronghold three times now. The last time he escaped, he sent two dragon guards to another time and place. No one has seen them since, and the king declared them both dead. After that the ice dragons were really out to get him. They'd be interested to learn what he's been up to lately."

Millie was changing back into a human even as she said, "Olebald turned Felix into a frog, Francis! He left him in a huge marsh in Soggy Molvinia. My brother is just a baby! He won't know how to find food or stay safe or anything! We have to find him right away, except we don't know how."

Francis reached up to scratch his head, and his fingers hit his helmet with a clang. He winced and shook his hand. "I want to help, but I don't know any frog-finding spells."

"Azuria, Oculura, and Dyspepsia are already looking for Felix. We think the best thing we can do is get my mother, only I don't know how to find the old witches' island. I was hoping you could tell me where it is."

"I don't know, either. My parents have gone there a few times, but they've never taken me with them. Is there anyone else you can think of who might know?"

"Great-Grandmother, but she's away with Great-Grandfather. There are probably some older witches in the retirement community who know, but I hate to waste time going door-to-door asking for directions."

"We might have to do that," said Francis, "unless . . . Does your mother still have the old carpet that used to belong to my mother? You know the one I mean—they used it the first time they flew to that island looking for Great-Grandmother."

Millie nodded. "It's in the back of her closet. At least it was when I went in looking for the basket with my old baby things. Mother saved all my clothes for when I have a baby, but she's using them for Felix now."

"You can use the carpet to find the island," said Francis. "Just tell it to take you to where it took your parents."

"That was a long time ago, Francis. My parents weren't even married then."

"Magic carpets never forget," said Francis. "I think it has to do with the way they're woven."

"It's worth a try," said Audun.

"I'll help you get the carpet started, then I'll see if I can locate a spell that would help me find a particular frog in a marsh full of frogs. But I think you're right; our best chance to find Felix is if your mother comes back."

❧

Emma's storage room was nothing like Millie's. True, they were both small and dark, but Millie usually tossed things into her room, then had to hunt around for them later. Her mother was much more organized and kept her storage room so neat that it was easy to find things. Millie located the rolled-up carpet leaning against the wall in the back of the room, a thick coating of dust dulling the vibrant colors on the outside. She could have sworn it shivered when her fingers brushed against it, almost as if it couldn't wait to go flying.

The carpet was heavier than the one her mother had given her, and it proved to be much bigger once Audun and Francis wrestled it through the door and unrolled it. The scarlet, gold, navy blue, dark green, and cream were brighter than Millie remembered. She had ridden on the carpet with her mother when she was younger, but Emma had used it only rarely.

The old carpet would seat four people easily. Two heavy cords were attached to the carpet next to where the people riding in the front would sit. Grassina had put them there the first time Emma and Eadric had ridden on the carpet without her, but Millie had no idea how to use them.

"It's awfully big," said Audun, scratching his chin as he studied the magic carpet. "Will it fit through the window?"

Millie nodded. "When I rode on it with my mother, the window widened to let us through. Have a seat," she said as she stepped onto the carpet and sat down cross-legged.

"You don't happen to remember what your mother used to say to get this carpet to move, do you?" asked Francis as Audun joined Millie.

"Not really," said Millie. "She hasn't used it in a long time."

Francis shrugged. "It probably doesn't matter much. The older magic carpets are kind of funny that way. It's more the magic and the intent behind it than what you actually say. I know something I can use that should work. Are you all set?" When Millie and Audun both agreed, he raised his hand in a dramatic gesture and said,

Take them to the island
That her parents went to see
When looking for the witches
Who had gone through trickery.

The magic carpet shivered just as it had in the storage room, only this time Millie could feel it through her whole body. When it rose from the floor, the movement was so smooth that she might not have noticed if her eyes hadn't been open. Audun took her hand as the carpet rose higher, and she turned and smiled at him. He'd been so helpful ever since he arrived. She didn't know what she would have done if he hadn't been around when Felix disappeared. Just having him there was—

The carpet suddenly darted forward, only to slam into the sides of the window frame. Millie cried out as she nearly fell through the window, but Audun had a good grip on her arm. He pulled her back as the magic carpet backed up and prepared to try again.

"No! Stop!" shouted Francis.

"Hold on!" Audun cried, grabbing the edge of the carpet with one hand and wrapping the other arm around Millie's waist.

Taking hold of one of the heavy cords attached to the carpet, she gripped it so hard that her knuckles turned white. The carpet quivered and took off, ramming the window frame with even greater force than before. Millie and Audun bobbed back and forth like a pair of children's toys, but they didn't fall.

"Jump off!" Francis ordered.

Frantic, Millie looked around. The carpet was already backing up to the rear wall. Then suddenly it shot forward and was nearly halfway to the window when it tilted onto its side. Millie and Audun grabbed the upper edge and held on, their feet scrabbling to get a purchase on the now-vertical carpet. This time it slipped through the window with room to spare, although both Millie and Audun scraped their legs against the windowsill. Once outside the castle, the carpet righted itself and took off into the cloudless azure sky.

"Be careful!" Francis called after them.

Millie glanced back, but the carpet was moving so fast that the castle was already dwindling in the distance. They were passing over the closest village when she let go of the cord and reached for Audun's hand.

"Tell me about the island," he said. "What was that about witches going there through trickery?"

"It happened before I was born," said Millie. "Olefat Wizard, Olebald's brother, tricked some witches into going to a tropical island. Some of the witches liked it there and decided to stay. Cadmilla, the witch who came to get Grassina, is one of the few who still lives on the island."

"I visited a tropical island once," said Audun. "It was too hot for my taste."

Millie laughed. "Most tropical islands probably are."

Although Millie had flown great distances as a dragon, she'd never grown tired of seeing the countryside change beneath her. She leaned forward now, watching the land below them. They flew past the Purple Mountains, where she'd often attended the Dragon Olympics with her friend Ralf and his parents. When she saw pink clouds rising from the volcanic bowl where dragons practiced flame-breathing events, she smiled and pointed it out to Audun. "I'll take you there to look around sometime," she said. "We can go to the Olympics, too, if you can stand the heat."

Millie's muscles became stiff long before they reached the desert, and she leaned back to watch the clouds. After a while her eyes closed and she dozed, waking with her head nestled against Audun's shoulder in time to see the sky turn red and orange as the sun set. Night came and they watched the twinkling stars. They talked about their plans for the future, and the constellations above, but mostly about Felix and what they hoped Emma would do when she returned to Greater Greensward.

They drifted off to sleep, and when they woke they were flying over the ocean. Ralf's parents had brought her to swim in the great rolling waves and she'd always loved the way it smelled. She sat up now, breathing deeply, and felt Audun's gaze on her. He was still lying down and she turned her head to look at him. The warmth of his gaze made her blush, but she smiled at him, happy to have him along.

They both turned their heads at the sound of wings. A gull landed on the edge of the carpet. It tilted its head to eye them, then took off, leaving a single feather behind. "There must be land around somewhere," Millie said, although she looked in every direction and couldn't see anything but water.

"There are lots of islands," said Audun, covering his mouth as he yawned. "The trick is finding the right one."

They saw the occasional islands after that, but the magic carpet passed each one, heading farther and farther south. There were no clouds in the sky, and the sun seemed to burn brighter with each passing minute. Millie began to look at the water with longing, imagining what the cool depths would feel like on her hot skin.

She was considering tearing off a strip of fabric to protect her face from the sun when suddenly the magic carpet shuddered to a halt, flipped over, and dumped them off. "Help!" Millie screamed, tumbling head over heels. The skirt of her gown flapped in her face each time she turned right side up so that she had to fight to see where she was headed.

She turned over so that she was upside down for a moment. Her skirt gathered around her legs, allowing her to see Audun falling only a few yards away. "Change!" he shouted as the air began to shimmer around him.

When Millie flipped again, the fabric slapped her in the face; she shoved it out of the way and glanced down. The sight of the water rushing up at her with incredible speed was nearly paralyzing. The crack of Audun's wing beat made her whip her head around so that she was looking away from the water . . . and then she changed, too.

Millie's feet were aimed toward the water when her first wing beat cupped the air, pushing her higher. The next few beats carried her past Audun, who was flying so close that the scales on his wings brushed hers. "I was going to catch you if you didn't change in time," he said, his brow wrinkled with worry.

"Do you know what happened? Why did we fall?"

"I have no idea," said Audun. "One minute we were flying along just fine, and the next the magic carpet was flipping upside down. I see an island ahead. Do you suppose it's the one we wanted?"

"Do you think the carpet flipped on purpose? My mother told me that she and Father turned into frogs and fell off the carpet. I guess it brought us to the same spot where my parents got off. I just wish we'd had some warning. You don't see the carpet anywhere, do you? I'd hate to lose it."

"I think I saw it headed back the way we came," said Audun.

"Maybe it's going home. Mother might have put a homing spell on it in case it got lost or stolen."

"About that island . . ."

"That might be it," Millie said, squinting into the bright sunlight. "It certainly won't hurt to go look."

They flew to the island, startling a flock of seagulls headed in the same direction. Millie peered down at the ground, looking for the witches, but there wasn't anyone on the beach or among the trees or anywhere on the island as far as she could tell. She circled around again and saw some debris just inside the tree line, but no sign of any people. Green crabs scuttled out of her way as she glided to a landing on the white sands of a pristine beach and raised her head to look around. Audun landed beside her, raising a cloud of sand with the last beat of his wings.

Millie closed her second eyelids until the sand settled. "I didn't see any people from the air, did you?" she asked.

"Not one," Audun replied. "And there's no sign of humans near the water. Maybe this isn't the right island after all."

"But this was the closest island to where we fell off the carpet. This should be it."

"Are you saying that because you have a feeling or because you want it to be true?"

"Both, I think," said Millie. "Because if this isn't the right island, I don't know what we're going to do!"

"I think we should look around some more," said Audun.

"Fine, but we don't have much time. If this isn't the right island, we have a whole lot of ocean to search."

Eight

I t's not a very big island," said Millie as she followed Audun up the beach. "I would have thought we'd see someone right away. If there are any people here, they should have noticed us by now."

"I'm sure your parents would have come running if they'd seen us."

"Grassina and Haywood would have, too. I don't understand. Where is everybody?"

"It *must* be the wrong island," said Audun.

Millie watched a crab scurry under a fallen log. "Then how are we going to find the right one?"

"I can fly very high and look for islands from up there," said Audun. "If there are any more nearby, I should be able to see them."

"If there aren't any clouds," Millie said. "You know, we could go talk to those seagulls we just saw. They live around here and would know where to find the islands." She noticed a little crab sitting on top of another fallen log, waving its eyestalks as it watched the two dragons. Millie took a step toward the log. "Do you think these crabs might know something?"

"Maybe," said Audun. "Catch one and we'll see."

The crab began to scuttle off the log as Millie reached for it, but she was quicker than the crab and caught it between her talons. She was careful not to hurt the little creature, but the crab squirmed and tried to pinch her scaly arm as she carried it back to Audun. Millie looked up at a sudden rustling sound. A small sea of green was washing across the sand, from under logs and rocks and out of trees. Crabs seemed to be coming from everywhere, clacking their claws threateningly. A bird with a black-tipped orange beak that was nearly as big as its all-black body flew out of the trees with a raucous squawk.

As the crabs reached Millie and Audun, they swarmed up the dragons' legs and onto their bodies, jabbing with their claws and trying to pinch the scale-covered skin. The bird flew straight at Millie and landed on her head, where it pecked her with so much force it gave her a headache.

Millie cried out and shook her head, trying to dislodge the bird. It squawked and flapped its wings, but she couldn't get rid of it. She was trying to whack her body with her tail when she glimpsed Audun, who was also under attack. A crab that appeared to be bigger than the rest was tossing coconuts at him; he would have been able to dodge them better if he hadn't been covered with green crabs. Another crab picked up a coconut and hurled it at

Millie, hitting her on the tip of her nose. She blinked and took a step back toward a patch of fallen palm fronds. Another coconut hit her right between the eyes. Jerking her head away, she took another step onto the palm fronds and felt her feet slip out from under her.

Audun roared as Millie slid down a steep incline and fell over onto her back in a space barely wider than her body. Water partially filled the hole, and she had to hold her head as high as she could to keep her nose in the air. The crabs scrambled off her, scuttling up the incline to peer down at her from the edge of the hole. Water seeped from the walls and she began to worry that it might soon cover her. She was struggling to turn over in the narrow space when a flurry of sand showered down on her; the crabs were trying to bury her in the hole. Millie dug her talons into the wall, stopping when she saw that her efforts were bringing down more sand and water.

She pressed her lips together until they were thin lines. No crabs were going to get the best of them! Taking a deep breath, she blew a stream of flame at the wall, melting it so that it turned into a layer of glass, made rough from the still-falling sand. The glass steamed as she tried to right herself, making the rising water slosh. The sloshing water touched the glass, cooling it so that it hardened.

Pushing against the glass, Millie turned over and clambered out of the hole. She no longer cared if she hurt the crabs or not, so she swatted them aside when they tried to swarm over her again as she reached level ground.

"Audun!" she called and heard an angry snarl in reply. She turned in the direction of the noise and saw him curled up on the ground, nose to tail, with ropes made of vines wrapped around him.

"Are you all right?" she asked as she hurried to his side, but the vines were wrapped around his muzzle, too, so he couldn't answer.

She noticed movement out of the corner of her eye and turned to see more crabs scuttling her way. Once again she took a deep breath and exhaled a tongue of flame, this time drawing a line of fire right in front of the advancing crabs. The little creatures immediately turned and ran toward the waves creeping up the shoreline.

"Hold still," she said, turning back to Audun. Grasping the vines with her talons, Millie pulled them as far from his body as she could and exhaled a trickle of flame. One tug and they broke in two. She had to do it to three more vines before Audun was able to shrug all of them off and get to his feet.

Millie glanced up. The crabs had gathered around a pile of fallen logs while the birds watched from the trees. "Have you ever heard of crabs acting this way before?"

"I don't think so," Audun replied. "But then, I don't know much about crabs."

"My mother used to have a crab friend named Shelton, and I always thought he was nice. He even looked like these crabs, but they don't act anything like him. Look at the way they're watching us."

"That's odd," said Audun. "Do you see those logs? They look like they've all been cut to the same length."

"Maybe they didn't fall down," she replied and started toward the pile of logs. When the crabs clacked their claws at her, one small puff of flame made them retreat to the edge of the water. Audun reached the logs before she did and began to rummage through them. Each log bore a smooth cut at either end. Some were notched and a few had vines tied around them. They found logs that had been bound together with vines as well as sheets of tied-together palm fronds.

"These were huts," said Millie, holding up a piece of a crudely made door.

Audun nodded. "Someone definitely lived here," he said and placed a cracked cooking pot by her feet.

"Then it may well have been where the witches lived. What do you suppose happened to them?"

"I don't know," said Audun. "Someone either chased them off or ate them."

Millie shivered. "I doubt they were eaten! They're witches, after all. I'm sure they could find some way to protect themselves."

"What do you want to do now?"

"I don't know. Except—we've looked at this from a dragon's perspective, but maybe we should look at it through human eyes."

"Why? Do you think it will look different?" asked Audun.

"Not really, or at least not much. But I know when I'm human, I think of things differently. You don't have to change if you don't want to."

Audun shook his head. "We might as well both do it. But what about the crabs?"

"We can always turn back if we need to," said Millie. "On the count of three. One, two, three . . ."

The first thing Millie noticed after changing back into her human form was the heat. High temperatures never bothered her when she was a dragon, but now she felt as if she'd been stuck in an oven as the hot sun reflected off the heated sand. The only thing keeping it from being unbearable was the breeze blowing off the ocean, but even that was warmer than she was used to in Greater Greensward. Perspiration beaded her forehead as she turned to face Audun, and she noticed that he seemed to be suffering even more.

"So far, I'm not enjoying this perspective very much," he told her. "I was hot as a dragon, but at least my entire body didn't sweat."

Millie wiped her forehead with the back of her hand. "I wish we had something cold to drink. There must be drinkable water on the island somewhere if the witches were able to live here, but I don't know how we'd find it."

"There's a small stream that leads into a pond behind those trees," said a woman's voice. Millie's eyes grew wide as she turned to where the crabs had retreated to the edge of the water. Seven witches stood there now, their hair scraggly and unkempt, their tattered clothes hanging on their thin frames. They all looked tired, as if they had gotten little sleep, although their sun-bronzed skin kept them from looking unhealthy.

"Cadmilla?" said Millie, recognizing the witch who had come to Greater Greensward to ask for Grassina's help.

The old witch gave her a sad half smile. "We didn't recognize you when you were dragons. We'd heard rumors that there was a princess who could change like that, but we didn't know it was you. We wouldn't have trapped you if we'd known."

"You were the crabs?" asked Audun.

"And the toucan," said a witch with a long face and a very thin nose. "I think I made a good toucan, don't you, Septicimia?"

A witch with wild-looking eyes nodded and clasped her hands. "You were the best, Rugene!" she said in a breathless voice.

"But why?" asked Millie. "And where are my parents and great-aunt and great-uncle? Did they already head back to Greater Greensward?"

"Sit down, dear," said a kindly looking witch. "I'm afraid we have some bad news for you."

"I'd rather stand," said Millie.

"Suit yourself," Cadmilla told her. "Remember that monster I told you about?"

"It came at night when we were asleep and destroyed our cottages," said Rugene. "We were lucky to get out with our lives."

Septicimia wrung her hands in front of her chest. "It has these long tentacles, and it uses them like whips. It flung my poor Henrik all the way across the beach and into the ocean. He didn't stand a chance."

"He was a fish in a bowl. He just went back where he came from. I doubt he minded all that much," Cadmilla said.

"I took good care of him," wailed Septicimia. "I loved him and he loved me!"

"I'm sure he did," said Rugene.

Cadmilla sighed. "The sea monster comes every night when the moon is highest in the sky. After it destroyed our cottages, it still came back looking for us. We hid at first, but it crossed the island and we had to climb the trees."

"It was Septicimia's idea that we turn ourselves into crabs."

"The monster didn't bother us when we weren't human anymore," Cadmilla told them. "But we didn't want to spend our entire lives as crabs or birds, and we didn't want to leave the island. We were very happy here until the sea monster came, so we built our traps and waited for it to come back. We haven't seen it in a few days, though."

"When you showed up, we thought that the sea witch had sent you after us, too," said Rugene. "Our traps worked very well, don't you think?"

Both Millie and Audun looked puzzled. "What sea witch?" they asked at the same time.

"The one that rode the sea monster," said Cadmilla. "Did we forget to mention that?"

"We're not telling this very well," said the kindly faced witch. "You see, my dears, a sea witch came with the sea monster. She was a mermaid and her scales were the most ghastly shade of green."

"We told your aunt about the sea witch and her monster. She said that she knew what to do and left," Cadmilla told them. "Then your mother came and we told her exactly what we'd told your aunt. She took off right away, too."

"But what happened to my mother and Grassina? Where are they now?"

"That's the bad part, dear," said the kindly faced witch. "Your aunt never came back, and neither did your mother."

Millie swallowed hard and her voice shook when she spoke. "And my father and great-uncle? What happened to them?"

"Your uncle went with your aunt and your father went with your mother, of course," said Cadmilla. "They're all missing. I wouldn't be surprised if the sea monster ate them."

Nine

illie didn't believe that the sea monster had eaten her family, despite what the witches said. Although she was sure they were in trouble, she was just as sure that they were still alive. "Call it dragoness intuition if you like, but I know we can save them if we hurry," Millie told Audun.

"What do you want to do? We can start looking for the sea monster. Perhaps some sea creature can tell us where it went when it left here."

"I guess that's what we'll have to do," said Millie. "Your amulet will work for me, too, won't it? I'll be able to breathe underwater like you can?"

"As long as we're touching," said Audun. "But we should go as dragons. We'll be much faster, and there's no saying what we'll run into down there."

"I hope we run into the sea monster," Millie said. "And I'd much rather be a dragon when we meet."

"Imagine that," said Rugene, who was still standing right there. "Being able to turn into dragons. It's amazing what young people can do these days."

"When I was a girl," Septicimia said, "I had a friend who tried to turn herself into a dragon. She changed partway, but it hurt so much that she got frightened and quit trying."

"Does it hurt when *you* change?" asked Rugene.

Millie laughed. "Not at all, although my mother said it hurt the first few times she did it."

"Do you mind if we watch?" asked Rugene. "I know we saw you turn back into humans, but it took us by surprise. Seeing you turn into dragons, well, I won't pretend I'm not curious."

"We don't mind," said Millie. "Just stand back. We wouldn't want you to get squashed by accident."

Septicimia gasped and the witches scurried back to the edge of the trees, then turned around to watch.

"They didn't need to go that far," Audun whispered to Millie. "What do they think we're going to do, turn into whales?"

"They'd probably enjoy that, too," said Millie. "We need to hurry and start looking, so let's do this together. One, two, three . . ."

They had gotten good at timing their turns at the same moment. The air began to shimmer around them, then their bodies began to elongate, their heads stretched, their limbs grew. Scaly skin replaced human flesh, and their teeth grew long and sharp. Their blinking eyes became larger, their pupils narrower. It all happened quicker than three heartbeats, and then they stood on the beach, water swirling around their scaled legs as their tails lashed the sand.

The dragons took to the air with the sound of the witches' applause. Millie could still hear them as she and Audun flew out over the curling waves to the deeper water that moved in small, barely discernible swells.

"Hold on tight," Audun said, taking her front talons in his.

They dove into the water and began to make a circle around the island. Millie held her breath until she remembered that it wasn't necessary. She felt a flutter of panic as she took her first breath, and relaxed when it felt natural.

Millie had gone swimming in the ocean as a dragon before, but she never grew tired of seeing what lay below the surface. Brightly colored fish darted around fantastic formations of coral, scattering as the dragons approached. Snaggle-toothed eels peered out from their hiding places, backing away when the dragons came too close. Large fish watched warily, keeping their distance. A curious shark came close enough to study the swimming dragons, then swam lazily away as if it had nothing to fear.

After swimming around the island once and seeing no hint of a sea monster, Millie and Audun expanded their search, swimming in ever-widening circles. As they moved away from the island, they no longer saw coral or the brightly colored fish, yet there was still life in the ocean around them. A strange flat fish nearly buried in the silt of the ocean floor watched them with one eye as they passed overhead. Fish as long as Millie's leg swam past in a school, their silver sides flashing as they changed direction. A huge crab scuttled across the ocean floor, leaving a trail of disturbed silt in its wake. And still they saw no sign of a sea monster.

They widened their circle, spiraling out from the island, which had now disappeared from sight. With nothing to use as a visual reference, Millie was glad that dragons had such a good sense of direction. No matter which way she turned, she knew where the island lay and even which way she'd have to fly to go home. Once she'd visited a place as a dragon, she could always find it again.

Lost in their own thoughts, Millie and Audun swam side by side in silence. That was one of the things that Millie liked most about Audun: he was great company even when neither of them had anything to say. She glanced at him and thought again how handsome he was and how good to help her with her family's problems. Most of the human princes she'd met would have helped her only if they themselves would have benefited in some way. Audun had told her that he did it simply because he loved her. She couldn't think of a better reason.

The ocean floor had begun to look monotonous, so Millie couldn't help but notice the seaweed. It started out as a few stray clumps but soon became a vast bed of long green plants swaying with the movement of the water, like saplings in a strong wind. Knowing that anything could lurk in the seaweed made her more cautious, but Audun plowed ahead, pulling her with him as they entered the forest that reached from the ocean floor to the water's surface.

The seaweed surrounded them immediately, muffling sound and blocking much of the light that filtered down through the water. Millie didn't like the way the seaweed hissed like a nest of baby snakes as it brushed against her scales, plucking at her limbs like long, green fingers. Even worse was the knowledge that some terrible beast could be only yards away and she wouldn't know it. She pulled her legs tighter to her body and discovered that she could swim faster with her legs tucked close and her tail moving from side to side to propel her. Powerful beats of her tail shoved the seaweed aside, tearing out the more persistent strands.

When they entered a thicker patch of seaweed, Millie felt increasingly anxious. She hurried Audun along, although they couldn't see where they were going. The only thing that kept her from panicking was having Audun close and hoping that nothing would want to take on two dragons at once.

They were racing through the seaweed when it ended suddenly and they emerged from the forest in a flurry of torn plants, nearly swimming into a mermaid. She looked terrified when she saw two dragons; turning tail in a swirl of long silver and dark blue hair, she sped away with only one quick backward glance.

"I know that mermaid," said Millie. "That's Coral. She's a friend of my mother's and Grassina's. I didn't realize we were so close to where she lives. Do you suppose my mother went to her for help?"

"It makes sense if your mother knew that her friend was close by. Maybe we should—"

"Let's go talk to her," Millie said, tugging at Audun.

"Did you see which way she went?"

"This way!" she said and let go of his talons to race after the mermaid.

"Millie!" cried Audun just as she realized what she'd done.

She turned and looked at him, suddenly all too aware of the weight of the water bearing down on her and that she had no air to breathe. Millie wanted to call out, but she stopped herself from trying, knowing that she'd lose her air that much faster. Although she could have held her breath for a few minutes and reached the surface with ease, it didn't occur to her to try. The only thing she wanted was Audun with his amulet. She couldn't believe how fast she'd become dependent on a small metal disk. Throwing herself toward him, she met him halfway.

"Don't let go!" he told her, pulling her into his arms.

Millie took a deep breath and smiled. "I won't!" she promised and kissed him, then turned and looked for

Coral. She saw the mermaid disappearing over a rise in the ocean floor. "Look," she said. "There she is."

This time Millie kept hold of Audun as they followed Coral. They were skimming over the rise when the mermaid stopped to look back. She shrieked and raced off to a castle visible in the distance.

"Wait!" Millie shouted, but the mermaid swam faster.

The two dragons followed her to the castle, reaching it while she was pounding on the door. Turning around, she brandished a long, pointed object that Millie thought looked like a unicorn's horn. "Stay back!" cried Coral, jabbing the horn in their direction. A stream of sparkling bubbles shot out of the horn, nearly hitting Millie and Audun as they lurched out of the way. The bubbles struck the rise with a loud boom, sending up a cloud of silt and debris.

"We just want to talk to you!" Millie screamed, but her voice sounded faint even to her own ears.

Coral aimed the horn at them again; they were already backing away. When the door opened behind her, the mermaid darted through the opening and slammed the door.

"That went well," said Audun. "Now what do you suggest?"

"I have to talk to her," Millie said. "But she's afraid of us when we're dragons. We have to let her see us as something a little less threatening."

It was the first time Millie had changed while touching anyone, and she wasn't sure she liked the feeling of someone else's hand altering its skin and shape while hers was doing the same. The contact also seemed to amplify the normal feelings and left her whole body tingling, like a foot or hand does when cut-off circulation is restored. Fortunately, the change seemed to go faster than usual, and she and Audun soon stood in front of the door as humans.

Millie was still feeling peculiar when Audun raised his fist. "Please let us in!" he shouted, pounding on the flat white surface. "Hurry, it's urgent!"

The door was a fragment of a giant seashell and had a single small bubble marring its perfect surface. Millie didn't remember the bubble being there, although it had been years since she and her mother had last visited the mermaid, so she leaned in for a better look. An eye suddenly appeared in the bubble, startling her so that she jerked her head back. The eye examined her for a moment before shifting to the side to study Audun. A moment after the eye disappeared, the door opened and Octavius, Coral's octopus butler, beckoned them in.

"What are you two doing out there?" he asked, sliding aside as they stepped across the threshold. "This is a terrible time to come visiting. There are monsters around and who knows what else."

"It's me, Octavius," said Millie. "I'm Millie, Emma's daughter."

The octopus looked at her as if he was affronted. "I know who you are, Princess. Didn't I dandle you in the highest tower of this castle when you were just a hatch-ling? Wasn't I the one who spent hours chasing you around the castle while your mother talked about magical things with Mistress Coral? And how many times did I have to undo the knots in your hair because that low-life crus-tacean Shelton hid there when we were playing hide-and-seek? I'd better warn you, Princess, he's getting ready to molt and is in a nasty temper."

"Shelton's here?" said Millie.

"And where else would he be?" Octavius asked, glid-ing down the floor in front of them. He was moving at an angle, as if the floor wasn't level, something Millie attributed to his age. "He's been here ever since your mother gave him to Mistress Coral, a dark day for us all."

"Shelton is the crab I mentioned before. My mother introduced him to Coral," Millie whispered to Audun. "They hit it off right away and Coral invited him to live with her. He came from the island where the witches live. He must be awfully old by now."

"You thought I was dead!" squeaked a voice by her elbow. "What a horrible thing to say about somebody! Although living here with that bloated bag who calls him-self a butler would be enough to shorten anyone's life. Did you know that he kidnapped me the other day and tried to stuff me down a hole in the ground bubbling with super-hot steam? I was lucky to get away with only a few toasted toes!"

103

"I wouldn't have done it if you hadn't glued my suckers to an electric eel, you vermin on a half shell. I'll probably list to the side for the rest of my life, shortened as it will be from living with you."

"Now, boys," said a melodious voice from another room. "How many times have I told you that I want you to get along? Who was at the door, Octavius?"

"Princess Millie and her friend," Octavius replied. "I think he's a very close friend, too. They've been holding hands ever since they arrived."

"Really?" said Coral, swimming into the hallway. She looked surprised and nearly dropped the seashell she was using to comb her long hair. Millie saw that the mermaid had already changed the seashells she wore on the top part of her body. "Ordinarily I'd be delighted to see you, but this isn't the best time for a visit. You didn't happen to see two horrible dragons when you came in, did you? I just had a very narrow escape! They were outside the castle a few minutes ago. I shot at them with my narwhal tusk. I put a repelling spell on it to keep the sea monster away, and I'm so glad I did. We've had such a terrible time of late. First the sea monster and now the dragons; who knows what's going to show up next?"

"Uh, should we tell her?" Audun asked Millie.

"I think we'd better," she told him.

Coral looked puzzled. "Tell me what?"

"That *we're* the two horrible dragons," said Millie. "I can turn into a dragon at will now, and Audun, well, he's a dragon who learned how to turn into a human. We didn't mean to frighten you. We just wanted to ask you some questions."

Coral clapped her hand over her mouth. "I'm so embarrassed!" said the mermaid. "I know that your mother can turn into one and I'd heard that you could, too, but it never occurred to me that you might be one of the dragons outside my door! And you're Audun? Grassina mentioned you. You're a very brave young man—er, dragon—from what I've heard. Octavius, what are you doing?"

One of the octopus's long tentacles was edging across the floor, reaching for Shelton, who was too busy listening to Coral to notice. Octavius stopped now and flushed a deep red. "I was about to take out the trash?"

"You two will never stop, will you? Why don't you get us something to eat, Octavius? You must be starving," she said, turning to Millie and Audun. "I'm sure becoming a dragon takes a lot out of you."

"Actually, this isn't a social visit. We need to ask you about my mother and Grassina. They came to help the witches who live on an island near here. Did either of them come to see you by any chance?"

Coral sighed and nodded. "I was afraid that was why you were here. Come sit down and I'll tell you what I know, which isn't much, unfortunately."

Millie looked worried when she glanced at Audun and was grateful when he slipped his arm around her. They followed the mermaid into another room and sat down on a bench made of polished stone. Coral sat down opposite them and lowered her hand to pick up Shelton, who was tugging at her tail.

"Grassina and Haywood stopped by first," said Coral. "They said that a sea witch was using a sea monster to terrorize some other witches on an island. I told her that the only sea witch in the area, other than myself, of course, was Nastia Nautica. I haven't seen her in ages, and since her daughter, Pearl, moved away, I haven't heard a word about her. I assume Nastia still lives where she always has. Her shipwreck isn't far from here—just on the other side of the seaweed. Grassina left after I told her that, and I haven't seen her since, but a few days later your mother and father showed up asking the same questions. I told them what I'd told Grassina, and they took off in a tremendous hurry. I was hoping they had taken care of their business and gone home, but to tell the truth, I was getting worried. If everything was all right, wouldn't they have stopped to say good-bye?"

"I'm sure they would have," said Millie. "But everything is not all right. They never came home and the witches never saw them again. We need to find my mother. Olebald Wizard kidnapped my baby brother, Felix, and turned him into a frog. He set him loose in Soggy Molvinia and we don't know how to get him back. Mother needs to come soon, before an animal eats Felix or steps on him or something equally horrible! And now my parents and great-aunt and great-uncle have all disappeared and are probably in terrible trouble, too. Whatever happened, I need to go help them and take them to Soggy Molvinia as soon as I possibly can!"

Ten

e should start by talking to Nastia Nautica," said Millie. "Two dragons should be able to handle one nasty sea witch."

"I'll go with you," Coral said. "If you'll give me a few minutes to get ready, I'll show you the way."

Audun shook his head. "That won't be necessary. I've already visited her sunken ship. I should be able to find it without any trouble."

"But you'll still have to deal with Nastia Nautica herself," said Coral. "She's usually horrible to everyone, but if she's the one behind the sea monster attacks, then she's gotten worse. You need me to go with you."

"If you really think you should . . . ," Millie said. "It's awfully kind of you to offer."

"Kindness has nothing to do with it. I've been a friend of your great-aunt and your mother long enough to know just how upset they'd be if anything bad happened to you. Oh, and take Shelton with you, in case we get separated. You can always send him back to me if you need my help."

"A fat lot of good he'd do," muttered Octavius.

"That will be all, Octavius!" Coral snapped at her butler. "You may go."

The octopus looked deflated as he slunk out the door, his eyes turning to watch them as he left.

"I don't know if Shelton will want to go with us," Millie said. "We'll be going as dragons."

Shelton waved his claws in the air. "I'm not afraid of dragons! See here, I'm wearing my own suit of armor! Nothing can hurt me." He thumped his shell with his claws and tried to look fierce.

"I didn't think you'd be afraid," Millie hurried to say. "It's just that we'll be traveling very fast, and you might be in danger when we meet Nastia Nautica."

The little crab scuttled down Coral's fishy tail, across the white sand-strewn floor, and up the skirt of Millie's gown. "When do we start?" he asked.

"Octavius!" Coral called. The octopus appeared in the doorway as if he'd been listening in all along. "Our guests and I will be leaving now. Please see that there's nothing lurking outside the door that shouldn't be there."

"Right away!" said the octopus, and he disappeared from view.

"Thank you for your help," said Millie. "We'll come back to visit you properly when we have more time."

"Just take care of that baby brother of yours," Coral told her. "Olebald Wizard is a horrible old man to have kidnapped a baby like that. And to turn him into a frog . . .

The least I can do is help you find Grassina and your mother. Now, if you'll give me just a minute, I'll go get ready."

Octavius made them wait while he peered through the bubble, then went outside to look around. When he came back and reported that the area was clear, he blocked their way with spread tentacles and said, "Good luck finding your parents, Princess. I like your mother. She was always nice to me, even if she did bring that pest Shelton here."

"Who are you calling a pest?" Shelton asked, peering out from Millie's cupped hands.

"Thank you, Octavius," Millie said before the crab and the octopus could start arguing again. "I'm sure we'll find them." She tried to swim over Octavius's raised tentacle, but the octopus refused to budge.

"And as for you," Octavius told Audun, "I've known this girl most of her life. I'm holding you responsible for her safety. You take good care of her, or you'll have to answer to me."

"She'll be fine," said Audun, and he tried to brush past the octopus, but the creature was strong and Audun couldn't move him.

"Promise me you'll take care of her," said Octavius.

"On my honor as a dragon," Audun told him, looking into the octopus's two wandering eyes.

Apparently satisfied, Octavius slid out of the way, letting Millie and Audun pass. They waited until the octopus had shut the door before they turned back into dragons. Shelton was excited to watch the transformation and even more excited to ride on a dragon's back. Millie let him sit between two of her ridge bumps, warning him to hold on tight, but he squirmed so much that she began to wonder if it was a good idea.

The door opened and Coral swam out wielding her narwhal tusk. She looked startled to see the two dragons, but quickly composed herself enough to say, "It is you, isn't it?"

Millie smiled in what she hoped was a reassuring way. "It's us, Coral. We're ready if you are."

The mermaid eyed their linked talons and frowned. "Are you going to hold hands while you swim? I should think that would make it more difficult."

"The only reason we can breathe underwater is because Audun is wearing an amulet that the ice dragon council gave him," said Millie.

"I see. You have only one amulet, so you have to share," Coral said with a knowing smile. "Very good. Now follow me." She led the way toward the seaweed, stopping to part the long strands with the tusk. "There's a trick to this. You don't want to just barrel ahead, because you never know whom or what you'll run into. Swim slowly and as quietly as you can; that way you won't attract attention to yourself and you'll hear if anything else is swimming through the seaweed." The mermaid slipped between the swaying plants, gesturing for the two dragons to follow. "I'd avoid this area altogether if I could," she continued, "but Nastia Nautica lives just on the other side and it would take too long to swim all the way around. This patch goes on forever. Well, not really, but if you get lost in it, it will certainly seem that way."

The mermaid stopped to poke something with her narwhal tusk, continuing on a moment later. "I was swimming through here once when I ran into an electric eel. It was quite a shock, believe me!" She turned around to see their expressions and seemed disappointed when they weren't laughing. "That was a joke," she said, facing forward once again. "I've never actually run into an electric eel, although I do have a friend who did. Her hair was straight before the incident and curly afterward. Her tail has a bad twitch now, too. Tsk! Such a shame."

Millie gritted her teeth, biting back a comment about people who talk after telling everyone else to be quiet. How were they supposed to hear something creeping up on them or even swimming in their direction if Coral wouldn't stop talking?

Suddenly the sound of hissing seaweed grew louder, and the mermaid stopped. Millie caught a glimpse of a narrow fishy face and a mouth filled with sharp teeth. A moment later the creature was racing away, leaving Coral screaming, "Stop! No! Come back here!" She swam off a little way, then rushed back to say, "A barracuda stole my narwhal tusk! I'll be back as soon as I can!" And then she was gone in a flurry of thrashing tail and tattered seaweed.

"I feel like we should go help her, but—," said Millie.

"She'll be fine," Audun told her. "We have something more important to do now. I've visited Nastia Nautica's shipwreck before, so I know the way."

"So do I," said Shelton. "It's over there."

Millie had forgotten that he was riding on her back ridge, and she curled her neck around to look at him. He was pointing straight ahead with one of his claws while holding on to her ridge with the other.

Audun looked annoyed. "I know. I told you I've been there before."

"Dragons have a fantastic sense of direction," Millie said, glancing back at Shelton. "For instance, Greater Greensward is that way." She pointed over her shoulder, then turned and pointed off to the right. "And the island where you grew up is that way."

The little crab climbed to the top of her ridge for a better look. "How do you know?" he asked. "Can you see that far?"

Millie shook her head. "We just know. Isn't there anything you know without seeing it?"

"Lots of things," said the little crab. "Like I know when Octavius is pretending he's mad and when he really is mad. And I know when I'm about to start molting. I should start in a few days. That's when I'll have to hide from that lousy butler."

The dragons swam with confidence, even when they had to change direction to get around a large rocky outcropping. When they finally emerged from the seaweed, they could see the shipwreck only a dozen yards away.

They approached the shipwreck slowly and without speaking. Eels slipped through gaping holes in the wooden walls. A large, flat, diamond-shaped creature swam past, dragging a whiplike tail behind it. Two small sharks circled overhead, leaving when they spotted the dragons.

"The last time I was here, Nastia Nautica was in a room at the back of the ship," said Audun.

Millie swam with him to the flattened stern and peered in the hole that had once been a window. Old sea chests sat against the walls alongside a wooden desk covered in barnacles. Tiny fish swam around and around in a tall, narrow glass jar that rested on the desk. A crooked bed occupied the corner, the bedding long gone. In the center of the room a high-backed chair faced the window, the perfect spot for someone to sit and watch the creatures of the sea swim by.

"She isn't here," said Millie.

"Maybe she's in another part of the ship," Audun said. "There was a big hole in the side. We can look in there."

They swam around the ship and peeked into the biggest hole, but there was nothing there except barnacles and a few fish that darted away. Peering into the other holes proved no more productive, and they wound up going to the far side of the hulk, where it rested at an angle on the ocean floor. When they peered through a small hole, they saw a big space with rotting barrels and crates jumbled on one side of the slanted floor.

"This wood is really decayed," said Audun when the piece next to the opening crumbled at his touch. "We could bash our way through if we really wanted to get inside."

"And let everyone for miles around know we're here?" Millie said. "What we need is someone small who can be discreet when he sneaks in and looks around."

When the two dragons turned to look at Shelton, the little crab jerked his eyestalks back and said, "You don't mean me, do you?"

"We wouldn't dream of asking . . . ," said Millie.

"He would," Shelton said, waving his claw at Audun.

"You *did* come along to help," Audun said.

Shelton grumbled as he released his hold on Millie's ridge. He swam toward the hole, gripping the edge with his claw, then turned to look back at the dragons. "I'm going, but if anything happens to me, it's your fault. Tell me, what exactly am I supposed to look for? You don't really expect me to find Nastia Nautica lurking in the hold of the ship, do you?"

Millie shook her head. "No, but since she doesn't seem to be here, now is a good time to look around. See if you can find something that will tell us what happened to my parents and my great-aunt and great-uncle."

"They might even be in there," Audun said, poking his head in partway. "If they are, I'll bash in the side and we'll get them out before the old sea witch gets back."

"You don't think she's kept them prisoner in there, do you?" Millie asked. "Hurry, Shelton! Go see if you can find them!"

Shelton disappeared from sight, reappearing now and then as he investigated the nooks and crannies in the hold. He swam back a few minutes later and said, "There's nothing here, but I saw another section up front. I'll go see what's up there."

"Hurry!" Millie urged the little crab as he swam off. "Nastia Nautica could be back any minute."

The ship creaked, making Millie back away in surprise. "Is it about to fall apart?" she asked Audun.

"Don't worry," he said. "Wrecks always make noises like that."

"But this one looks like it's in awfully bad shape."

Audun stepped back to take a long look at the hull. "It's been here for years and will probably be here for many more to come. Unless there's an earthquake or something, I don't think—"

"Come quick," Shelton said, so excited that his voice was little more than a squeak. "I found the sea monster in the front part of the hold. We'll find a way for you to get in and . . . Oh yeah. That'll work, too," Shelton added as Audun turned and pulled his tail to the side.

There was a loud boom as the dragon hit the hull with his tail, rocking the ship and creating a hole big enough for an enormous shark or a medium-sized dragon to pass through. Some of the debris rained down around Millie and some flew back into the hold, covering the tops of the barrels and crates. There wasn't room for them to swim side by side, so Millie held on to Audun's tail ridge as he

116

swam the length of the hold. He knocked aside everything that got in his way, shattering crates and barrels that
had stayed intact over all the years that the ship had sat at
the bottom of the ocean. Millie swam through clouds of
sour-tasting pickle juice and long-fermented wine, around
broken pottery and maggoty bread. When they reached the
far end, Audun turned to face her in the cramped space
and swung his tail as best he could, bashing another
hole in the wall.

At first Audun's body blocked her view, but when he
moved farther into the next room she could see the sea
monster as well. It was just as Cadmilla had described it,
with its warty body, three flippers, and tentacles with leaf-
shaped tips. What the witch hadn't mentioned was that it
was bigger than four dragons Audun's size put together and
that it had two soulful-looking eyes like a puppy. Despite
its size, the monster didn't look the least bit threatening
as it lay cowering under Audun's fearsome glare.

"What did you do with the Green Witch and her family?" Audun roared.

The sea monster shrank back as if it had been struck.
Its sacklike body quivered, sending ripples from one end
to the other. "Urp!" belched the monster.

"Don't play innocent with me!" said Audun. "I know
you've been terrorizing an island of witches. What did you
do with the Green Witch?"

When Audun took a step closer, the sea monster fled to
the wall, its flippers carrying it in an uneven rush to a hole

117

no bigger than an ordinary loaf of bread. Squeezing one flipper through the hole, it oozed out, dragging its weight until it plopped through on the other side. Audun rushed to the wall with Millie close behind, but the monster was already swimming like a sea slug as it undulated out of sight.

"Should I go after it?" Audun asked.

"I don't think there's much point," said Millie. "I don't think it's fearsome enough to have attacked the witches on its own. Nastia Nautica must have been controlling it. She's the one we have to find."

Shelton had climbed back onto Millie's ridge. "Maybe Coral knows where else you could look," he said.

"We can go ask," Audun said with a sigh.

They were leaving the gloom of the wreck when Millie had the strongest feeling that something was watching them. She glanced back at the ship but didn't see anything peering out. The seaweed could have held an army of sea creatures, but nothing was making itself obvious. "I think something is here with us, but I don't see anything," she told Audun in a whisper.

"I do," he said, looking at the ground beside the ship.

Millie's eyes opened wide. Black lines that she had thought were cracks in the ground seemed to be wiggling. She rubbed her eyes with her front foot and looked again. The lines were coming closer, and as they drew nearer, they seemed to widen and take on features that . . . Millie realized with a start that they were sea snakes—

hundreds and hundreds of sea snakes. She watched as they rose up from the ground and swam toward them.

Millie backed away, ready to flee, but when Audun didn't move, she turned to him and stopped, her mouth hanging open. The snakes were swarming around him, making happy little sounds.

Audun looked just as happy to see them. "Hello, my friends! It's good to see you again, but why are there so many of you?"

"We stayed here waiting for your return," said one of the sea snakes. "Our friends and relatives came to join us once they learned that you had set us free. We are here to serve you, Great One."

"I don't have the flute anymore. I thought you helped me before only because I had the flute."

"When the flute left the ocean, we could no longer protect it and the spell was broken forever," said another sea snake. "We do not wish to serve you because we have to, Great One, but because we want to. Tell us, what can we do to help you?"

"I'm looking for some humans—two men and two women," he told the sea snakes.

"We don't know if they are men or women, but we do know where there are some humans," said a snake swimming past Millie's ear.

She shrank back, but it was paying no attention to her. When she glanced at Shelton, she noticed that he was holding on to her ridge with one claw while the rest of him was hiding in his shell.

"There are humans on the island and humans in your old cave," a sea snake told Audun.

"But you shouldn't go near any of them," said another.

"The humans on the island scream and run away when we swim past."

"And no one can get near the ones in the cave. The entrance is too dangerous."

"Our cousin tried to go in and was squashed when the roof to the tunnel collapsed."

"Two other cousins went in as well. We warned them to be careful, and they were. They didn't touch the tunnel walls, but more of the roof collapsed anyway."

"They were squashed, too."

"And what about the humans inside the cave?" asked Audun.

"They yelled when the roof collapsed, which only made it fall down more."

"Thank you, my friends," Audun said. "You've been very helpful."

"We have?" said one of the sea snakes.

"Indeed," Audun told them. "You have repaid whatever debt you believe you owe me."

"But we want to serve you, Great One!"

Audun thought a minute, then said, "Then wait here for my return, but live as you would anywhere else."

"Ooh," said one of the snakes. "We can do that!"

When Millie and Audun left, the snakes were writhing with happiness. Millie couldn't get away fast enough.

Audun obviously knew where he was going when he headed for the seaweed again. "We won't have to be in here long this time," he told Millie. "The seaweed doesn't grow very far in this direction."

"I assume my parents and Grassina and Haywood are the humans in the cave," said Millie, "but that doesn't make sense. My mother, my great-aunt, and my great-uncle all have magic. Why can't they get out? Unless . . . Oh, Audun, you don't suppose they're dead, do you?"

"I don't think that at all," said Audun. "You heard what the sea snakes said about the humans shouting when the tunnel roof collapsed. The tunnel is fairly long and the cave itself had plenty of room. They should be fine. As to why they can't get out . . . Do you remember the stones Olebald brought with him and tried to hide in the dungeon under your parents' castle?"

Millie nodded. "They were the same as the stones in the roc's nest. They prevented magic from working near them."

"The stones came from this cave. I saw them on the walls when Nastia Nautica tried to trap me in there. She must have given some stones to Olebald Wizard."

"So my family can't get out because their magic doesn't work. And the sea snakes say that no one can get in without making the roof collapse," said Millie. "We're going to need something to hold up the roof. Perhaps we could get some wood from Nastia Nautica's ship."

"That wood is too rotten," Audun said. "It wouldn't be strong enough to hold up the roof and support the walls for long. No, what we need is something strong that can hold up the roof from more than one angle."

"What can we use, then?" asked Millie.

"Not what, whom. And I know just whom to ask."

Eleven

It didn't take long for Shelton to return to the tunnel with Octavius. "I don't know why I have to do this," the octopus grumbled. "We could still go back to the castle and wait for Coral to return. I'm sure she'll be back soon, and with her magic you could—"

"Magic doesn't work in the cave," said Audun. "Or past the entrance of the tunnel. I know. I've been in it. We need you because you have all those strong legs. How many do you have, anyway?"

"Eight, but they're tentacles, not legs," Octavius said in a quarrelsome voice.

"Start at the front of the tunnel and work your way back to where the roof is weak," said Millie.

"Just leave room for us to get past," said Audun. "We'll have to haul out all the rocks that fell from the roof."

"Is there anything else?" asked Octavius. "I mean, if you want to stand here all day telling me what to do, I'll make myself comfortable and—"

"No, no!" Audun said. "That's all. You can go now."

"And be snappy about it!" Shelton said, snapping his claws like castanets.

Octavius turned one of his eyes toward the little crab. "Watch it or I might toss you into the tunnel to see if it's safe!"

Shelton scuttled behind Millie's tallest ridge and pulled his eyestalks into his shell. "Never mind!" he said and pulled the rest of himself inside, too.

Millie could hear Octavius grumbling all the way down the tunnel. When he stopped, he called back to them, "I found the first weak spot. Here goes . . . If I put one tentacle here and another over here . . . There's one there. I'll have to twist my body like this, but I might be able to reach it if I . . ."

"What are we going to do if he can't reach them all?" Millie whispered to Audun.

"I'm not going to worry about that unless I have to," Audun told her. "Let's just hope he doesn't run out of tentacles."

"All right!" Octavius called after a few minutes. "I think I have them all. You can come in now, but don't touch the walls and don't bump me, or the whole thing might come crashing down."

Audun entered the tunnel with Millie close behind, holding on to his tail. It was nearly pitch black inside the tunnel, but Millie could see with very little light. She followed Audun's example and hunched down so that she was practically crawling on her knees. And then the tunnel got narrower and she *was* crawling. "Does it get any narrower than this?" she asked Audun.

"A little," he said. "But unless it's collapsed so much that we can't get through, we should be able to fit."

"That's encouraging," Millie muttered. "Ask Octavius if he can see anyone in the cave."

"I can hear you," said the octopus. "You can talk right to me, you know. I can't see anything from here, but if I twist this way a little . . . Nope. All I can see are rocks. I can try calling if you want me to. Emma! Eadric! Grassina! Grassina's husband whose name I can't remember!"

"He's my great-uncle and his name is Haywood," said Millie.

"Yeah? Well, it doesn't really matter. No one is answering me, anyway."

"Is there an opening big enough for Shelton to fit through? Maybe he can see inside the cave."

"Unh-unh," Shelton said. "You're not getting me to go up there until the opening is big enough for you. I'm not getting trapped in a cave when the tunnel collapses!"

Millie sighed. She was growing more anxious by the minute.

The sound of rock scraping on rock reached her ears. A moment later Audun pushed a pile of stones to her. Without letting go of his tail, she shoved the stones back with her feet, wishing she had longer legs to shove the rubble out of the tunnel. She glanced back to see how far from the entrance she had to carry them and saw something moving in the near dark.

"We have come to help, oh friend of the Great One," said a sea snake.

"In what way may we assist you?" asked another.

"Can you drag these stones out of the tunnel?" Millie asked, tapping the rubble with her hind foot.

"Yesss," a group of them said at once.

"Who are you talking to?" asked Octavius.

"Sea snakes," Millie replied.

Stones clattered up ahead as if Octavius had shifted. "I hate sea snakes," he said just loud enough for Millie to hear.

Millie would have loved to watch to see how the sea snakes moved the rubble, but Audun was already passing more rocks to her. She passed them on, then the bigger rocks that he shoved back one at a time. When Audun crept forward, she did, too, and the whole process started over. No matter how far they moved into the tunnel, the snakes were right there behind her, clearing away the rocks.

After what seemed like hours, Audun reached Octavius and began to inch past him. Millie heard only bits and pieces of their muttered comments to one another. "If you don't move that tentacle, you're going to have only seven." "Watch where you put that thing!" "You want me to go where?" "Ow! Your scales are sharp!" "You're not nearly as slimy as I thought you were."

Millie was tired, her back ached from crouching down for so long, and she'd already broken two talons on rocks. She had tried to be patient, but worry was making her temper shorter. She wanted to snap at Audun and Octavius and tell them to hurry up, but that would just start an argument and not help anything. Finally, trying not to let her impatience show, she asked, "How far are we now? Can you see anything yet?"

"Didn't you just ask that?" said Octavius. "No, I still can't see a thing."

"But I've almost reached it," Audun told her. "I'm out of the water now. Just a few more feet . . . There," he said, half dragging Millie past the octopus and into the cave as he lurched clear of the tunnel. He reached down and drew her up to join him and they stood side by side, looking around the enormous cave. It was dark, with a dim, pale green light coming from the green stones embedded in the walls. Water lapped around their ankles as they stepped farther into the cave. The remains of plants that normally grew in seawater hung dead and limp on the walls, as if the cave had once been filled with water. A few fish swam in the water on the floor, but they darted away at the dragons' approach.

The walls of the cave were uneven and bore ledges of varying sizes. There were shapes perched on some of the ledges; some looked just like rocks, the rest . . . ?

"Mother?" Millie called, the word catching in her throat.

One of the shapes groaned. Another raised a hand a few inches before letting it fall back to the ledge.

"It's them!" Millie let go of Audun and sped across the cave to crouch beside one of the figures. "My father is breathing," she said and inhaled, but the air smelled stale and she found herself gasping after the first few breaths.

Shelton climbed down off her back and looked around, waving his eyestalks.

"They've used up most of the good air," Audun said, placing his hand on her shoulder. "Let's not use up the rest. We need to get them out of here before it's all gone. Grassina is breathing, too."

"And here's your mother," said Shelton, swimming through the water covering the floor of the cave.

"Are they all . . . breathing?" Millie asked, almost too afraid to say it.

"Barely," said Audun as he straightened up from beside Haywood. He pulled off the chain holding the amulet and handed it to Millie. "Here, put this on. You can take your mother and Grassina out first. I'll stay here with your father and your great-uncle."

"But you won't be able to breathe!" said Millie.

"There's a little good air left. Just don't take too long!"

"I'll be as quick as I can," said Millie. "Help me get them to the door."

With Audun's help, Millie was able to carry her nearly lifeless mother and great-aunt out of the cave and into the tunnel. It was difficult getting the two women past Octavius, but he proved to be exceedingly pliable, and after some maneuvering Millie was able to squeeze them through the narrow space.

Millie was anxious to return to the cave to get Audun and the men, but first she had to see the women to safety. Because she was wearing the amulet, both Emma and Grassina were able to breathe again and both began to get color back in their cheeks. Neither woman was conscious, however, which meant that Millie would have to lug two dead weights to the surface and drag them through the waves to dry land. Swimming with her front legs wrapped around bodies was a difficult process and took far longer than she would have liked.

She was nearing the surface when she felt the presence of something behind her. After checking to make sure that the women were still all right, she bent her neck to look down. A large figure was coming out of the darker reaches of the water; at first Millie couldn't tell what it was. It wasn't until she saw an old mermaid with dark eyes like bottomless pits and wild, nearly translucent hair that she realized it was Nastia Nautica, and the blob that kept changing shape beneath her was the sea monster.

Millie curled her lip in a dragonish snarl. Nastia Nautica had already tried to kill members of Millie's family; she wasn't about to give the sea witch a second chance. Thrashing her tail as hard as she could, she swept her hind legs back in a powerful swoop and shot through the water, carrying Emma and Grassina into the open air. She tried to open her wings with their usual snap, but the water slowed her so that she fell back with a splash.

Something latched on to Millie's ankle and she shook her leg; whatever was holding on to her was strong, and it began to drag her toward the ocean floor. She glanced down and saw one of the sea monster's tentacles wrapped around her ankle.

Emma stirred in her daughter's grasp as the sea witch laughed with glee. "This is even better than I planned!" Nastia Nautica chortled. "Give the witch hope of escape, then take it away again. I'd heard the Green Witch's daughter could turn into a dragon, but I never thought I'd catch her, too! Swim, you misbegotten son of a monster's worst dream!" she screamed, prodding the sea monster with a curved whalebone. "We'll stuff them back in the cave and shut the entrance for good!"

Millie looked down again as she jerked her leg back and forth, trying to get rid of the tentacle. The sea monster held on, but it seemed reluctant to yank at Millie. Each time it hesitated, however, Nastia Nautica used the whalebone prod, poking the monster between its sad-looking eyes. Wincing from the blow, the sea monster tugged on Millie again.

"Millie?" Emma said, her voice so faint that her daughter almost missed it. "Is that you?"

"Don't worry, Mother," Millie told her. "Everything will be all right."

Even as the sea monster dragged Millie down into the ocean's depths, she was thinking about something else entirely. She thought about the Dragon Olympics and how she had come in second after Flame Snorter, Ralf's mother, the previous month. She thought about how it felt when fire burned hot in her belly and flame scorched her throat. She thought about what it was like to aim the flame at one point, narrowing it so that it shot in a straight line that nothing could extinguish. And then Millie arched her neck to look down at the still-laughing sea witch, and she flamed.

A tongue of fire shot from between the dragon's puckered lips, aiming straight for the sea witch. The flame lit up the depths as water boiled around it. Nastia Nautica screamed and turned the sea monster so the fire hit it instead. The monster shrieked—an unearthly sound that seemed to echo in Millie's ears long after it ended. Blisters appeared on its shapeless body and it writhed, letting go of Millie's leg and sending Nastia Nautica tumbling. The sea witch screamed and once again Emma stirred in Millie's arms.

Pulling herself upright, Emma cleared her throat. She pointed at the flailing sea witch and said, "Now it's my turn."

Spin around and spin around
Then rise into the air
Form a twirling tower
That will whisk away the pair
Carry them across the sea
To a place no human dwells
Where crashing waves will keep them
   trapped
Beneath the rising swells

Water began to swirl around the sea witch and the
monster, catching them up and twirling them in an ever-
rising circle, which lengthened, becoming a water spout.
Millie backed away to watch the spout grow as it pulled
more water into its spiral. Within seconds it had reached
the surface and rose into the air, carrying Nastia Nautica and her monster with it. The monster cried out, a
plaintive sound that tore at Millie. She turned her head
aside, not wanting to see the look in the monster's eyes as
the water spout rose higher until it disappeared from
sight.

"Are they gone?" asked Shelton, peeking out from
behind Millie's tallest ridge.

Millie smiled. She hadn't realized that Shelton was there,
but she was delighted to see him. "Yes, they're gone, thanks
to my mother. But I have a job for you now. Take this amulet
to Audun," she said, pulling the chain off over her head.

"Tell him that we're fine and we're waiting for him here. Hurry! They didn't have much air left."

Shelton sighed and snagged the chain with his claw. "Why do I get all the dangerous jobs?" he said and turned to swim away.

Twelve

hen Audun broke the surface of the water hauling
Eadric and Haywood, who were pale but very
much alive, Millie was sure they'd all be able to start back
to Greater Greensward soon. The humans were still dazed
and disoriented, so she and Audun shouldered their
burdens and turned to the distant palm trees barely visible on the horizon. While the two dragons carried the
humans toward the island, their lashing tails propelling
them through the waves, Millie thought about what to do
next. They'd go to the island, and she'd give her parents a
few minutes to rest before telling them about Felix. Then
they'd all go home, find Felix, and everything would be
back to normal.

As they dragged themselves out of the water and onto
the beach, she told Audun that they'd be leaving soon and
that he needn't bother changing into his human form.
Unfortunately, the four former captives were exhausted,
ill, hungry, and desperately thirsty, so Millie waited as the
old witches swarmed around them, offering them food

and drink. When Millie tried to talk to her mother, Rugene shooed her away, saying that her parents needed to rest. Half an hour later, the women were still fussing over them, making sure that they had enough to drink and eat and were comfortable sitting on the witches' own feather mattresses dredged up from the nearly repaired ruins of their cottages.

Millie could scarcely sit still. She could feel the all-too-precious time trickling away like the sand she scooped from the beach where she sat beside Audun.

"Octavius feels terrible about what he did," said Audun, interrupting Millie's thoughts. "He told me so while we were waiting for you to come back."

"Why would he feel terrible? Without him we never could have gone through the tunnel to get them out," Millie said.

"He tried to talk us into waiting for Coral. If we had listened to him, all four of them might have died."

Millie shrugged. Any other time she might have worried about Octavius's feelings, but right now something else caused her far more concern. "But we didn't wait, so it worked out all right," she said. "He doesn't need to feel bad. I, however, feel lousy, and I don't see you worrying about me. I know that what you said was true—my mother asked me to watch over Greater Greensward *and* Felix, and I couldn't possibly be in both places at once, but I can't help feeling that I was still responsible. I was supposed to keep an eye on him and—"

"Do all humans fret this much?" asked Audun. "Dragons are much more sensible creatures. We don't dwell on what we did or didn't do, or at least not in our saner moments."

Millie's breath escaped with a gasp. "My brother was kidnapped by a lunatic and here you are calling me crazy! I can't believe that you would say such a—"

Audun shook his head even as he interrupted her. "I never called you crazy, nor did I mean to imply that you—"

"I'm not so sure about that," said Millie. "This is the second time you've told me how much better dragons are than humans. If that's really the way you feel, maybe we don't belong together. Maybe it's a good thing we haven't finished planning our wedding. Maybe we shouldn't have a wedding at all!"

Audun reached for her, his eyes stricken. "Millie, you can't mean that."

"I'm not sure if I do or not," she said, pulling away. "If you'll excuse me, I'm going to go try to talk to my parents again."

Millie walked away with her back stiff and her head held high. She was still upset as she worked her way through the group of witches to Emma, who must have seen the expression on her face because she stepped forward when Cadmilla tried to intercept the young dragoness. "Thank you for your hospitality," said Emma, "but I need to talk to my daughter."

Millie had thought long and hard about how she would tell her parents that their baby had been kidnapped. She'd wanted to break the news to them gently, but now, when she actually had to tell them, all she could do was blurt out, "I know you're tired and have gone through a terrible ordeal, but we have to go. I came looking for you because Olebald Wizard kidnapped Felix and took him to Soggy Molvinia."

Emma gasped and her hand flew to her mouth. She swayed until Eadric came up behind her and put his arm around her waist. "What's this about Felix?" he asked.

"Olebald Wizard kidnapped him," Millie said again. "He took him to Soggy Molvinia and turned him into a frog. The fairy Raindrop helped us follow him there, but he'd already released Felix into the marsh, where he's with a billion other frogs. Francis, Oculura, Dyspepsia, and Azuria are all looking for Felix, but Audun and I came to get you because I was sure that you would know what to do."

Eadric nodded and pulled Emma closer. "You did the right thing. We'll go there straightaway. Your mother can find anything, can't you, Emma?"

"Yes, but my baby! How could anyone do such a horrible thing? And of all the times for this to happen, why did Olebald have to do it now?"

"I think he was in league with Nastia Nautica," said Audun, who had come up behind Millie. He set his talons on Millie's shoulder and gave it a gentle squeeze. "They must have planned it together. She lured you away and trapped you in her cave while he kidnapped Felix. Who knows what else he has in mind?"

"That's right," Millie told them as she twitched her shoulder out from under Audun's touch and took a step away from him. "When Olebald brought the roc to Greater Greensward and tried to tear down the castle last year, he had green stones with him like the ones in Nastia Nautica's cave. If he got the stones from her, he must have known her for some time."

"We have to get to Soggy Molvinia as soon as possible," said Eadric.

"I have a spell that could carry us there in an instant, but it won't work on all six of us," Emma said.

"You two go, and take Grassina and Haywood," said Millie. "Audun and I will fly back. It won't take us long as dragons."

"We'll do that," said Emma, "but hurry. Olebald has obviously been planning this for a while. It sounds as if he's already wielded more powerful magic than I've ever seen him use before. I don't know if I'll be able to undo his spell. If that's the case, we're all going to be searching the marsh for Felix."

Millie and Audun left the island just as her mother raised her hand and waved it in the air. In the next instant, the magic carpets and their riders vanished. The dragons turned and headed toward Soggy Molvinia, flying without talking for the first few miles. "I didn't mean that you were crazy," said Audun, finally breaking the silence. "I just wish you'd stop worrying so much. Worrying never helped anyone."

"But my baby brother has been turned into a frog!"

"I know, and we're going to take care of it. You've already done so much. You discovered that Olebald took Felix and that he put him in the marsh. You've also found your parents, and now they're on their way back to the marsh. No one blames you for any of this."

"My mother might, when she really thinks about it," said Millie.

Audun quirked one eye ridge at her. "Do you really think so? From what I know of your mother, she's a very practical person. I think she'd be the last one to blame you for what happened to Felix. Now, I've never met her, but I'd bet that your grandmother Frazzela would be happy to blame you, especially when you're a dragon."

Millie laughed. "Yes, and your grandmother Song of the Glacier would probably blame me when I'm a human. I don't know what we're going to do if they both show up for the wedding."

"You mean there is going to be a wedding even after I stuck my talons in my mouth?" Audun said.

"Yes, there will be a wedding," Millie said, smiling. "Everybody says things they don't mean when they're upset."

Audun looked relieved. "I know, and you were upset even before—"

"I wasn't talking about me!" said Millie. "You're the one who said what he shouldn't have. Just don't do it again," she added with a warning look.

When Audun closed his mouth with a snap, Millie couldn't help but smile.

They made good time flying over the ocean, but as they approached the shore, they saw dark, ominous-looking clouds looming over the land. "We could go around," Audun said as lightning split the sky only a few miles in front of them.

Millie shook her head. The clouds stretched as far as she could see in both directions. "It looks like an awfully big storm. Going around would take too long."

"We can try to go above the storm, although those clouds look enormous."

"Then we'll just have to go higher," said Millie.

Flying wingtip to wingtip, she and Audun spiraled upward, trying to gain altitude without entering the clouds. As the storm drew nearer, the air became rougher, buffeting them back and forth until Millie felt sick to her stomach.

"Just a little higher," said Audun, yet the clouds appeared to go on forever.

Millie looked around as lightning crashed so close that the air seemed to sizzle. The clouds surrounded them on all sides; when she looked up again, what had been clear sky above them was dark and ominous.

"I don't like this," Millie said, watching the clouds above them grow thicker.

"I don't, either," said Audun. "Let's get out of here. How fast can you fly?"

"At least as fast as you!" Millie told him.

They raced—first the lightning, then the torrential rain, and then, after they passed through the storm and out the other side, they raced each other. Neither one was faster, and they didn't stop until they had passed the border into Soggy Molvinia and the marsh lay just ahead.

"We're almost there," Millie said, glancing down at the first of the ponds that riddled the marshy land. Puddles, ponds, lakes of all sizes, and the thin ribbon of land that wound between them made patterns of light and dark in the pale haze of morning. If it hadn't been for their dragon senses, they might have become lost in minutes, but they flew on, landing on the same hillock where they'd spoken with Olebald Wizard.

When they'd left, three witches had been searching for Felix. Oculura, Dyspepsia, and Azuria were still there, along with Emma, Eadric, Grassina, Haywood, and another witch named Mudine. Oculura and Dyspepsia were stomping around the edge of puddles and ponds, poking through the mud as they looked for frogs, while everyone else was gathered around Emma and Eadric. The two dragons changed back into their human form before approaching the group, and Millie was about to call to her mother when the air sparkled in front of them and the Swamp Fairy appeared.

"I found some more," she said, jerking her thumb at two bewildered men who had appeared behind her. They were well dressed, although their clothes were out of date and didn't seem to fit very well. One crouched down into a squatting position and the other shivered and looked around, apparently too stunned to move.

"Let me question them before they join the others," said Eadric, breaking free from the group surrounding Emma. He noticed Millie and Audun then, and his lips shaped themselves into a weary smile. "There you are. We were beginning to worry about you. Before you ask—no, no luck so far. Talk to your mother, Millie, so she can fill you in."

Millie nodded. "I will, but first tell me, where's Francis? He said he was going to come here to help search for Felix."

"He was here," said Azuria, "but a fairy came to get him. She said he was needed at home. They went back to Greater Greensward together, and we haven't seen him since."

"That's odd," Millie muttered as she went to join her mother.

Emma looked even more tired than Eadric, with dark circles under her eyes and her brow etched with worry lines. She glanced up as the witches made room for Millie and Audun to pass. "I'm glad you're here," she said, running her fingers through her hair, making it messier than before. "I've tried everything I can think of, including the spell that I used to find Haywood when he was an otter, but none of my locator spells have done what they should and my summoning spells have been worthless. There were some other princes here, as you can see." She waved her hand at a group of men huddled together on another hillock. They looked as bewildered and just as out of place as the two the Swamp Fairy had found. "Unfortunately, Felix wasn't among them. Your father has been questioning the princes, but none of them know anything about my baby boy. There's only one thing left to try," said Emma. "I'll have to go look for him as a frog."

"Not without me, you're not," said Eadric from behind the witches. He worked his way through the group and took Emma's hand. "I've spent more time as a frog than you have. I know how to get other frogs to talk to me."

"And I'm going, too," Millie told them both. "He's my baby brother and I was in charge while you were gone."

"Actually," said Eadric, "you and Francis were in charge of magical problems. It was your grandparents who—"

"Yes, you can go," Emma said. "But stay near us. I don't want to lose both my children in this marsh."

"I can go, too," said Haywood. "Just turn me back into an otter and I can find any frog!"

"If you were an otter, you'd scare away every frog for miles around and we'd never find my baby," said Emma.

"Thank you for the offer, but I'd rather you stayed here and helped Grassina coordinate the witches' search. You could keep all the predators out of the marsh, too. The last thing we need is for a real otter to eat one of us while we're looking for Felix."

"Are you sure?" asked Haywood. "I could keep the other predators away better if I were an otter. Turn me back and I'll stay away from the frogs. I'd turn myself back, but I never did perfect the spell."

"I can't believe I'm saying this, but I'll turn you into an otter, Haywood," said Grassina. "Just be careful and stay out of the way."

Millie had never been a frog before. She was a human most of the time and she loved being a dragon, but it had never occurred to her to try anything else. Turning into a dragon had never made her nervous or anxious. Now, however, the thought of turning into a frog made her stomach churn, and she began to wonder if she was doing the right thing.

"Where should we look first?" Eadric asked Emma.

"I'm not sure," she replied. "That big pond over there looks promising, or we could try this one."

"We should try the one on the other side of that little hill where Audun and I met Olebald," said Millie. "I have a feeling about that pond."

Audun glanced at her, then turned to her parents and said, "You should trust her feelings. She's developing good dragoness intuition that has proven to be right more often than not."

"But she's not a dragoness now," said Eadric.

"Millie is a mixture of dragon and human," Audun said. "It seems the line between what she can do when she's one or the other is getting a little blurred."

"That pond is as good as the next," said Emma. "I think we should go with Millie's choice. Audun, I'd appreciate it if you could help Haywood keep the predators away."

Audun smiled, but he didn't look happy. "As the biggest predator around here, I'd say I'm very qualified for the job, but I can probably do it better from the air."

After trudging across the narrow strip of land connecting one hillock to another, Millie and her parents took up positions facing one another. "We should hold hands so the spell includes the three of us," said Emma. "Now, be friendly when you meet other frogs, so they'll talk to you. We're more likely to find Felix quickly if the frogs who live here are helping us."

Millie was already reaching for her parents' hands when the air shimmered around Audun and he changed into a dragon. She turned back to face her parents when her mother began the spell.

> Green of skin,
> And long of tongue,

With strong bespeckled feet.
Turn us into
Three fine frogs
That others want to meet.

Perhaps turning back and forth between human and dragon so often had made it easy for Millie, but for whatever reason, there was no pain or discomfort, and it happened so fast that she didn't think it had happened at all until she glanced down and saw that she was green and smooth and much smaller than either of her other usual forms. She blinked in surprise as her mother patted her hand with long green fingers.

"Follow us while you practice swimming," Emma told Millie. "I don't want to have to look for you, too." Then taking one hop backward and twisting her body halfway around, Emma jumped into the water with a tiny splash.

Millie shook her head in disbelief. Her mother knew that she could swim perfectly well as a human and even better as a dragon. Millie had been doing it for years and— She fell flat on her face, her long, thin feet tangled together. "Ow!" she exclaimed, rubbing the spot where she normally had a nose. Millie tried again, tugging until she'd freed her feet, then moved them carefully, one slow step at a time.

"It's not as easy as it looks, is it?" said her father. "Don't worry, you'll get it soon enough. Your mother didn't catch on right away, and neither did I, for that matter." He turned to look out over the water and frowned. "Where did she go? I'd better go find her. We'll meet you in the middle of the pond." Her father's splash was even smaller than her mother's.

Millie thought about hopping the way her parents had, but she couldn't manage more than a stumbling lurch. She ended up walking flat-footed to the water, then inching her way in until she was waist deep. Stretching her arms in front of her, she belly flopped into the water and kicked her feet. Her long legs felt awkward and uncomfortable, and she didn't go far.

Someone nearby began to laugh, a deep-throated sound that managed to seem good natured, even though Millie was sure the person was laughing at her. "I've never seen anyone do it that way," said a big bullfrog popping up beside her. "It helps if you bend your legs. No," he said when Millie tried, "not like that. Like this!"

Millie watched as the frog bent his legs to the side and straightened them with a thrusting motion. He sped past, waving at her with one hand. "I can do that!" Millie murmured, bringing her feet closer to her body. She kicked the way she'd seen the bullfrog do and was delighted when she actually moved forward.

"You're funny!" said a little frog as it swam circles around her.

"She's new," another, slightly larger frog said.

"What pond did you come from?" asked the little frog. "Are you going to live here now?"

"Actually, I'm just visiting," Millie began. "I'm looking for my brother. Have any of you met a frog named Felix? He's been here just a few days."

A crowd of frogs had gathered around her, bobbing in the water so that all she could see were their heads, which looked very odd when they all shook them saying "No."

"Two other frogs just got here, but nobody came before them," said the bullfrog. "Maybe your brother is in another pond."

"Maybe," said Millie. "But I have a feeling he's here somewhere."

One of the frogs giggled and splashed Millie. "Did you hear that? She has a feeling!"

"I have a lot of feelings," said another. "But that doesn't mean anything is going to happen."

"I just meant that something is telling me he's here. I'd appreciate it if you could all keep your eyes open for a little frog named Felix."

"She wants us to keep our eyes open. As if we don't already! Who says things like that?"

"She's with those humans clomping around in the shallows," said a female frog as she joined the group. "They took my boyfriend! We were sitting down to a nice mosquito snack when *zap*—he turned into a great galumphing human! He always said he was a prince, but I thought he was crazy like Peto. That fool claims he's really a snapping turtle, although I can almost believe *him*."

A froggy face rose above the back of the crowd and grinned evilly at Millie. He opened his mouth and snapped it shut with a loud *clack*. Even Millie could see how much he resembled a snapping turtle.

"I'm sorry they took your friend, but if he was a prince, he didn't really belong here," Millie told the female frog. "We'll all leave as soon as we find my brother. He's just a baby, you see, and can't take care of himself yet."

"A baby, you say? You should have mentioned that right away," said the bullfrog. "Baby frogs aren't frogs. Well, they are, but that's not what we call them. We call them little squirts, although I've heard them called polliwogs and tadpoles."

"I like 'polliwogs' the best," said the little frog. "It feels funny in my mouth when I say it."

Millie was so stunned that she let her legs drop straight down and she began to sink. She came back up spluttering and wiping the water from her eyes. "I never thought of that!" she said. "But it makes a lot of sense! I have to tell my parents. Thank you so much!" She started to swim away, then stopped abruptly and came back. "Where exactly would I find these polliwogs?"

"They swim in big groups in the shallows," said the little frog.

"Thanks again!" Millie shouted as she started toward the middle of the pond.

"I said they're in the shallows," the little frog shouted after her. "You're going the wrong way!"

"I have to tell my parents first," Millie called over her shoulder.

"Suit yourself. Just watch out for Old Gray. He hangs out in the middle of the pond until the sun gets high."

Swimming as a frog still wasn't easy for Millie, but she tried the bend-and-kick style and found she actually made some progress with it. Every now and then she raised her head to look around and make sure that she was still headed where she wanted to go. Finally, she chanced to look down as well and saw a shadow following her.

Unfortunately, it wasn't her own shadow.

"What is that?" she wondered out loud and stuck her face in the water for a better look. The shadow moved closer until she was able to see that it was a fish, not a shadow at all. It was hard to judge how far away the fish was or how big it might be, but Millie remembered the little frog's warning about Old Gray and decided that she really didn't want to learn any more about him.

She tried to swim faster, pulling her legs closer and kicking harder, and began to move at a better pace. Even so, when she glanced back down, she saw that the fish was drawing nearer and looked more threatening than before. Millie tried to swim faster still, but she had already been doing the best she could and he continued to come closer. Her heart pounded and her limbs felt like they were on fire when she realized that the fish was rising to the surface and was only inches behind her.

"Help!" she screamed. There was a *whoosh* and something enormous tore out of the sky. Millie shrieked and shot ahead as Audun plucked the fish from the water. "Thank you!" she shouted once she realized that it was him and that he held the flopping fish in his talons.

"No problem," said Audun. "I was hungry, anyway."

"Millie, are you all right?" her mother shouted, and she saw both of her parents swimming toward her, their eyes big with concern.

"I'm better than all right," she told them, "because I know where we might be able to find Felix." Her eyes shone as she told them about her conversation with the frogs, and by the time she had finished they were already swimming to the shallows.

They swam through the cattails edging the shallower water calling "Felix!" but for the longest time they didn't see anything that even resembled a tadpole. "Maybe I was wrong and he is in a different pond," Millie finally said.

"We're not giving up yet," her father told her with an encouraging smile.

Millie ducked when a blackbird darted overhead, and she bumped into something small and soft. A tadpole looked up at her with curious eyes before scooting off through a stand of water iris. Millie followed, pushing aside the iris as she forced her way through, and swam into the midst of the largest group of tadpoles she'd ever seen.

Startled, the tadpoles darted away, moving together like one much larger entity.

"I found them!" Millie shouted, and her parents hurried over to meet her.

"Felix!" called Emma as she drew alongside the tadpoles.

"Are you there, Felix?" his father called.

Millie glanced from one tadpole to another and shook her head. "It's impossible to tell them apart."

"It is, isn't it? And none of them answers to 'Felix,'" said Emma.

"Maybe we should try something else," Millie said. "He's ticklish when he's human. Do you think he might be ticklish as a tadpole, too?"

Emma smiled. "What a good idea! When I was a frog, Grassina tickled me and knew who I was by my laugh. I doubt any real tadpole would laugh like Felix. You start at that end of the group and I'll start at this end. Eadric, can you work your way out from the cattails?"

"How will we know which ones we've checked already?" asked Millie. "I know some have little legs and some are bigger than others, but I don't think I can keep them all straight."

"Dab some mud on each one after you tickle it," said Eadric. "Unless you can think of a better way to mark them."

"Mud sounds good to me," said Millie, bending down to get a big glob.

Although Millie thought that tickling tadpoles might be fun, she changed her mind after the first few. Some tadpoles squirmed to get away, but most of them just gave the frogs bored looks and swam off. An hour had gone by and her froggy fingers were sore when a dark shape shot out of the deeper water, scattering the tadpoles in every direction.

"Hello!" said Haywood, his otter mouth grinning. "I came to see how you were doing."

Millie didn't know a frog could look as angry as her mother looked just then. "We were doing fine until you came and chased all the polliwogs away!" Emma said, her froggy eyes bulging even more than usual.

Haywood looked confused. "What do polliwogs have to do with . . . Oh, I get it. You think Felix is a polliwog now! That makes sense because—"

"We can talk about it later," snapped Emma. "Right now I want you to get those polliwogs back. Go on, round them up and send them back here."

Haywood ducked his head like a little boy who'd just been scolded. "Sorry," he muttered. "I didn't know. I'll see what I can do." He swam off and in less than two minutes a flood of tadpoles surrounded the three frogs.

"How did he do it that fast?" asked Millie as she reached for a tadpole.

"He probably used magic," her mother said, trying to tickle two tadpoles at once. "Small magic has always been his specialty."

Millie gazed out over the sea of tadpoles that didn't show any sign of leaving. "He must have sent us every tadpole in the pond."

"Good," said Eadric. "Then Felix should be here somewhere."

Millie was getting sick of the sight, smell, and feel of tadpoles when her father finally tickled one that chortled with glee. Eadric called Emma and Millie over to see the tadpole. They recognized Felix's laugh even before they saw him and were both grinning when they gave the little creature a froggy hug.

"Now we have to get him to shore without losing him again," said Emma as they all tried to hold on to the squirmy tadpole. "The problem is, we have to keep him in water until I can change us back. I'm afraid I'll drop him if I try to hold him while I change."

Eadric looked around until he noticed a depression in the mud at the edge of the pond. "We can trap him in a puddle," he said. "Millie, come help me. We'll build up the sides so he can't get out."

"Hurry!" said Emma with her arms wrapped around the tadpole. "I won't be able to hold him for long. He's too slippery!"

Working as fast as they could, Millie and her father splashed water into the depression, then slapped mud around the edges, building them high enough to keep in even the most determined tadpole. When it was ready, they helped Emma lug the wiggly little creature over the mud wall and dump him into his own private puddle. Millie glanced at her parents and laughed. They were covered in mud, and so was she.

"Step back, everyone!" said Emma. "I'm going to turn us back first, and we don't want to step on Felix."

Millie scrambled out of the water, adding another layer of mud to her arms and legs. The three of them moved away from the pond and took hold of one another's hands again. The spell that Emma used was one Millie had heard before, only this time it applied to her, too.

> Turn us into that which we
> long ago were meant to be.
> Make us human once again
> From head to toe and bone to skin.

Once they were human again, they stood beaming at one another for a moment before turning to look at the tadpole they were sure was Felix.

Emma knelt down beside the puddle to recite another spell.

> An evil man has turned my babe
> Into a polliwog.
> Change him back to the boy I love,
> A human, not a frog.

Millie waited, expecting the air to shimmer or lights to sparkle or something that would show the spell was working. Nothing happened, however, and the tadpole continued to swim in his little puddle.

"What's going on?" asked Oculura as the witches gathered around.

"Felix was turned into a tadpole, not a fully developed frog," said Emma. "I tried to turn him back, but my spell didn't work."

"Maybe you didn't say it right," said Dyspepsia.

"Mother always says it right and her spells always work," Millie told her. "Something else is wrong."

"Let me try," said Azuria.

Millie stepped aside as one witch after another tried to change the tadpole back. Standing by the pond, she let her mind wander. The pond had felt right, and now the tadpole felt right. That was Felix, she was sure of it. Whatever wasn't right wasn't anything they had done, it was Olebald. It had to be.

"Mother," said Millie. "Didn't you tell me that normally only the witch who cast a spell can undo it?"

Emma glanced at her and sighed. "Usually, yes, although I've been able to undo most witches' spells ever since I became a dragon friend. I was hoping that I could do it now as well, but it isn't working. The only one who can undo this spell is Olebald Wizard. We're going to have to find him."

Thirteen

They were flying over the enchanted forest when Millie slowed the beat of her wings so she could talk to her mother. Emma was riding on her magic carpet with Eadric, cradling the glass bowl that Grassina had created out of an old spell, a leaf, and a blob of mud. Pond water sloshed in the bowl, and the little tadpole swimming in the water sloshed with it.

Her mother was murmuring something to Felix when Millie appeared beside her. Emma glanced at Millie, then at Eadric, who was snoring softly, his head lolling at an angle. "My poor darling," said Emma. "He's exhausted. But then we all are today."

"Mother, I have to ask you, isn't your spell supposed to take us to Olebald?"

Emma was only half paying attention to Millie when she answered, "What's that, dear? Oh yes, that's right."

"But it looks as if we're going home," Millie told her. "I can already see the castle beyond the trees."

Emma frowned and looked up. "That's not possible," she said, her cheeks paling when she saw the castle. "This isn't good. It can mean one of two things; either my spell didn't work, or Olebald is here in Greater Greensward. I don't know which would be worse."

"If he's here, at least we won't have to go looking for him," said Millie.

❧

They made a strange procession as they approached the castle: two dragons, two magic carpets each bearing a man and a woman, and four witches on broomsticks. Gliding over the battlements, they were aiming for the courtyard, but they seemed to hit an invisible barrier in turn and bounced a little before sliding off the side like a speck of dust on a soap bubble. They all ended up outside the castle wall, looking confused.

"What's going on?" Millie asked Audun as they met in the air above the moat.

"I don't know," said Audun. "But there's your cousin, Francis. He's waving to us."

Millie spotted Francis standing by the moat dressed in his best suit of armor. It gleamed gold in the sunlight, making him hard to look at. "Good," Millie said. "He should know what's happening." She turned on a wingtip and headed toward her cousin.

"Did you find Felix?" Francis called before they were even close.

"We found him, but we still have a problem," said Millie. "He's a tadpole and we can't change him back. We need Olebald Wizard for that."

"I've been told that he's in the castle, but I haven't seen him yet," said Francis. "Grandmother and Grandfather saw him for a few minutes before I returned."

When Millie tilted her head to the side in a quizzical way, Francis sighed and said, "Perhaps I should start from the beginning. I was helping the witches look for Felix when a fairy came to tell me that my grandparents needed me here. I hurried back and found everyone outside on the road leading to the drawbridge. Olebald Wizard had used an illusion spell in the middle of the night to make it look as if the castle were on fire. Everyone, including the guards, fled the castle. Once everyone was outside, Olebald closed the drawbridge and ended his illusion. Now no one can get inside. Stand back and I'll show you something."

Millie and Audun stood well back as Francis nocked an arrow in his bow, took aim over the castle wall, and let fly. The two dragons watched as the arrow arched over the wall with a whistling sound, hit something with a *twang!* and came flying back. Francis ran to the side, but the arrow headed straight for him. He dodged to the other side and the arrow changed direction. When it looked as if he wasn't going to be able to avoid it, he turned around and braced himself. The arrow hit him in the center of his back with enough force to knock him off his feet. Millie wasn't too worried however, because she knew he'd made his armor puncture proof.

"I thought you'd given up shooting arrows over the wall, Francis," King Limelyn said as he, Queen Chartreuse, and Emma crossed the well-trodden path around the moat to join them. The king acknowledged Audun with a single nod and patted Millie on her scaly cheek. "I'm glad you're back. Your mother told me about Felix. Did Francis tell you what Olebald Wizard has done here?"

"He did," said Millie. "Francis also said that you saw Olebald, but no one has seen him since."

"After he closed the drawbridge, he came out on the wall walk to gloat," said the king. "When he saw us watching him, he did a little dance and laughed so hard he had to lean against a parapet so he didn't fall over. Then he shouted down at us, 'I've finally done it. You think you're so smart, but I'm smarter than all of you. This castle is mine now and there's nothing you can do about it.' I can't believe that the old cuss tricked us into abandoning our home without lifting a finger to stop him. That fire illusion had me convinced. It crackled and flared and looked so real!"

"You could smell it, too," said Queen Chartreuse. "That wizard is evil, but he's very good at what he does. I was terrified! Olebald is a horrible old scoundrel to have frightened us all so. Now that you're back, you must kick him out of our castle. It's disgraceful. No queen should ever be seen in public in her nightgown, but the fire started so suddenly that I didn't have time to change. "

"It wasn't a real fire, my dear," said King Limelyn.

"I know," said the queen, "but I thought it was, and that's what mattered."

"Have you tried to get in through the secret passageway yet?" asked Audun.

"It was blocked," the king told him. "My men have done everything from trying to batter the door down to hacking at it with axes. Olebald Wizard must have used magic to protect it, too. As for the walls . . . I've given up counting how many places where we've tried to scale the walls and been repelled each time, even though no one is there."

"I'll see what I can do," said Emma. "Millie, you and Audun can take a look at the secret passage while I see about the walls. There must be some way we can get inside the castle."

Millie and Audun weren't far from the secret passage, so it took them only minutes to get there. Brushing aside the concealing vegetation, they entered the tunnel and followed it back to the door. A broken ax sat propped against the wall, and the dirt floor was churned up from the passage of many feet, but the door itself was intact and looked the same as always. Banded in iron and at least a foot thick, the wooden door was meant to withstand just about anything.

Millie waited while Audun tried the latch. When he looked back at her, she raised an eye ridge and said, "I'm sure someone already did that."

Audun shrugged. "You never know," he replied. "Stand back. I'm going to try to knock it down."

"But the soldiers—"

"Aren't as strong as I am. I bet they never tried this."

Millie backed down the tunnel, leaving Audun enough room to turn around. Pulling his tail back, he let go and hit the door with a *whump*. The door shook and dust billowed through the tunnel. When Audun cried out, there was so much dust that Millie couldn't see what had happened.

"Are you all right?" she asked.

"Fine," Audun said in a grumpy voice. "My tail came back and hit me, that's all." He took a step backward and groaned. "I think I sprained it."

The dust cleared, leaving the door looking just as it had before.

"I don't understand," said Audun.

"Move aside, please," said Millie. "It's my turn now."

The two dragons squeezed past each other to change places in the narrow tunnel. Millie eyed the door, then glanced back at Audun. "On second thought, you should probably go outside. It might get awfully hot in here—not at all the place for an ice dragon."

Audun nodded. "I'll go, but I don't like leaving you alone."

"I know, and I appreciate your thoughtfulness," said Millie, and she blew him a kiss. She waited until the sound of his footsteps had died away before taking a deep breath. Millie preferred fueling her flames with gunga beans and hot flammi peppers, but she hadn't eaten any in days and her only supply was in the castle. Now when she needed her biggest flame the most, her ordinary flame would have to do. She thought about her flame even as she filled her lungs with air. It needed to be hot and last long enough to test any magic the old wizard could have used. Anything less would be a waste of her breath.

Millie held the air inside her until she could feel the flame build, then closed her second set of eyelids, stepped back, and aimed for the center of the door. Dragon fire washed over the wood long enough to turn it to ash. Flame caressed the iron bindings and thick hinges until they should have melted into pools of liquid metal. And still she flamed, willing the fire to last. And then the last bit of air left her lungs and she gasped.

Millie blinked her second lids open and examined the door. It looked just as it had before she started. The stone walls around the door glowed red, however, and when she touched one, her talon sizzled.

The fire she had blasted at the door had washed back over her. Fire didn't bother fire-breathing dragons, but she was glad Audun had left when he did. Ice dragons could get burned just like humans, although they were totally comfortable with ice.

"Princess Emma? Is that you?" called a faint voice from the other side of the door.

"No, it's her daughter, Millie!" shouted the young dragoness. "Who are you?"

"It's Sir Jarvis! Someone has done something awful to the dungeon. The ghosts can't pass through walls or doors anymore. We're trapped wherever we were at midnight last night. Poor Hubert is stuck between one cell and the next. I was fortunate enough to be in the corridor at the time. Can you come in here and do something about this?"

"I wish I could," said Millie, "but Olebald Wizard has tricked everyone into leaving the castle and we can't get back in."

"Then he's the one! That dastardly rogue! This must be his revenge for when we foiled his break-in last year."

"Or he wants to make sure you can't help us now," she replied.

"Millie!" Audun called and she could hear him approach from down the tunnel. "Is everything all right?"

"It didn't work," said Millie.

"And we ghosts are trapped!" came Sir Jarvis's muffled voice.

"Then I guess we won't be asking them for help," said Audun. "Millie, I think you should come now. I heard a lot of shouting at the front of the castle."

"I'm coming," Millie told him. She turned and yelled at the door, "Tell the other ghosts that we're trying to get in. We'll help you as soon as we can."

164

"Please hurry," said Sir Jarvis. "Hubert hasn't stopped moaning since he was trapped. We'd end his suffering if he weren't already dead, so now we're trying to think of a way to drown out the sound of his moans."

"I'll do what I can," Millie called over her shoulder as she started back down the tunnel.

She heard the shouting as soon as she stuck her head outside the tunnel entrance. Although she couldn't make out what they were saying, it sounded as if a large group of men were arguing. She and Audun ran down the moat path and arrived by the drawbridge just as a makeshift siege ladder, propped against the wall, began to fall backward. Soldiers clung to the ladder as their legs dangled over empty air. Millie flew up to grab hold of the ladder, but Emma was there first, and she held it still while Millie and Audun helped the men down.

"We have an idea!" Oculura shouted to the dragons. "Come talk to us."

Emma sighed. "You go, Millie. I have to see what your grandfather wants to do next. I've been trying to talk him out of digging a tunnel that would come up in the dungeon. You should thank me. He already asked me to dig it with magic, and if that doesn't work he wants you and me to use our talons, with Audun's help, of course," she said, giving the ice dragon a halfhearted smile.

"You can tell Grandfather that it wouldn't do any good," said Millie. "The ghosts are trapped in the dungeon and

I'm betting any human who ends up down there would be trapped as well."

Emma's smile widened. "I'll be sure to tell him. Maybe that will get him to stop asking. Oh dear, he's talking to Azuria now. He's probably trying to get her to do it. I'd better go. Be careful, darling. People are coming up with all sorts of ways to get into the castle, and some of them are very dangerous."

Oculura, Dyspepsia, and Mudine rushed over to Millie when she landed. All three witches were quivering with excitement. "We've had the best idea!" cried Mudine.

"It was my idea, actually," Dyspepsia hurried to say.

"No, I think it was Mudine's," said Oculura. "I think she should be the one to explain it to Millie."

Dyspepsia scowled. "Does it really matter?"

"What is this idea?" Millie asked.

"It's quite simple," said Mudine. "We think Olebald must be directing invisible servants to repel attacks from the air. They are probably looking for the more traditional siege weapons, like ladders and catapults. However, we think we could sneak in when Olebald is distracted by the catapult."

"What catapult?" Millie asked, looking around.

"The one your grandfather is building with Azuria," said Dyspepsia. "Haven't you been paying attention?"

"I've been busy," said Millie. "So how do you plan to sneak over the castle wall?"

"Millie, can you come here for a moment?" her father called.

"I'll be right there," she replied, then turned back to the three witches. "Don't go anywhere until I get back. I want to talk to you."

"Millie, it's important!" her father called again.

She hurried to where King Limelyn was standing with her parents and the witch Azuria. No one acknowledged her, however, because her mother and grandfather were in the midst of an argument and everyone standing nearby was listening. "I told you that the tunnel isn't a good idea," said Emma. "I can't believe you had Azuria dig it. The way was blocked just like every other way has been, and now we're going to have to fill it in."

"It would have worked if Olebald hadn't put a spell on the dungeon," said Azuria.

Emma frowned. "I told you about the spell."

"After we dug the tunnel!" said the king.

"I didn't know you had even started!" Emma sighed and looked toward the field where a catapult was being loaded. "And when did you find the time to build a catapult?" she asked Azuria.

"I did that before I dug the tunnel," said the old witch. "I do so want to be helpful."

"And have you thought about what is going to happen when you use that thing?" asked Eadric. "Think about the arrows the men shot over the wall."

"The range is much greater," said Azuria. "The men will be fine."

The king scratched his head and looked doubtful. "I hadn't thought of that. To tell the truth, my head is getting a bit muzzy. Lack of sleep, I suppose."

"Well, I don't think it's a good idea," said Emma. "We should— Oh no, don't tell me they've started already!"

Everyone watched as a boulder hurtled from the cup of the catapult and flew over the wall. There was a smack like a paddle hitting a leather-covered ball and the boulder flew back over the wall, heading for the catapult.

"Run!" Emma shrieked and began a hurried spell to get the men operating the catapult out of the way.

"I did tell them to begin as soon as they were ready," the king said.

The men scattered, moving twice as fast as was normally possible for an ordinary human, and were well away from the catapult when the boulder hit, smashing it to bits. Emma lowered her arms and sighed. "Is there anything else I don't know about?" she asked her father.

"No, just that—"

"What on earth are they doing?" asked Azuria, pointing at the wall.

Oculura, Dyspepsia, and Mudine had flown their brooms across the moat and landed on the thin strip of ground circling the castle. Millie watched openmouthed as Mudine finished whatever spell she was saying and all three witches flopped down on their backs. Raising their feet, they pressed them against the vertical castle wall and began to walk up as easily as if on level ground, although their bodies were sticking straight out to the side like quills on a porcupine.

"They're crazy!" said Eadric, and everyone else nodded.

Even though they took slow, methodical steps, it wasn't long before the witches reached the top. They were raising their feet to step between the parapets when a strong wind sprang up, hitting them full force in the face and blowing them over backward. With only one leg firmly attached to the castle wall, the witches flapped like flags in a storm and couldn't move until the wind died down. A moment later they were running backward down the wall, flailing their arms and shrieking.

"I told them to wait," muttered Millie. "Some people just won't listen."

Fourteen

Emma glanced down into the glass bowl and frowned. "I'm worried about Felix," she said, holding up the bowl. "He's no longer swimming the way he should. Look."

Millie peered into the bowl and her breath caught in her throat. Although the little tadpole had been darting from one side of the bowl to the other the last time she'd seen him, he was now moving lethargically through the water as if it had turned into thick syrup.

"This can't be good," she said, feeling the first flutter of panic. Her baby brother *couldn't* die, but he would if they didn't do something soon. "We have to think of a way to get to Olebald!"

"Excuse me, but I think they're having a problem undoing the spell," Azuria said, pointing at the castle wall. "Perhaps I should go help them."

The witches were lying on their backs at the base of the wall, struggling to remove the bottoms of their feet from the stone surface. "Let them work it out," Emma said to Azuria. "It will keep them out of trouble." She peered down into the bowl again and shook it just a little. "Maybe it will help if I change his water."

Emma was hurrying to the side of the moat when Millie turned to Audun. "I have an idea. Remember how the door in the secret passage shook when you hit it with your tail? What if I hit it harder—I mean really, really hard?"

"We might be able to get through then, but there isn't room in the tunnel for you to swing your tail any better than I did before."

"I don't plan to use my tail. What if I dive from high up and hit the air above the castle full force? I've found that when I fly high and let myself drop from the sky, I end up moving at tremendous speed, like a hawk. With tremendous speed comes tremendous force. If I were to hit whatever is keeping everyone from flying over the wall, I might actually be able to make it through. I bet it's the same magic surrounding the entire castle."

Audun shook his head. "That's too dangerous. It's practically suicidal."

"But it could work?"

"I guess so," he said, sounding reluctant.

"Then it's worth a try," Millie said and took to the air.

"Millie, you can't do this!" said Audun, following her with a mighty sweep of his wings. "I can't let you risk your life this way!"

"Aren't you the one who's been telling me that I can do anything?" Millie asked him. "I thought you wanted me to believe in myself. Well, I believe in myself now and I wish that you would, too. You have to give me the chance to prove what I can do, and I know that I can do this. Look, it's not like I'd be hitting a really hard surface. We sort of bounced when we tried to land in the courtyard."

"Even so, I don't think—"

"Audun, we have to do something, and no one has come up with anything better!"

The ice dragon sighed and glanced down at the castle, then up at the sky above. "My father's special talent is that he can fly very high. I'm nearly as good as he is, if I do say so myself."

Millie reached out and touched Audun's cheek with her talons. "You'd risk your life for my family?"

"I'd do anything for you, Millie," he told her.

"And I for you," Millie said. "But you don't have to do this. It was my idea and I'll take the risk."

Audun shook his head. "We're doing it together. Two dragons are better than one, after all. If you can damage Olebald's magic, imagine what we can do together."

"In that case, the last one there is a rotten roc egg!" Millie shouted and turned her face toward the clouds high above. She began to spiral upward with Audun at her side. Flying wingtip to wingtip, they rose high into the sky, until the castle was no more than the tiniest speck when they looked down.

"Is this high enough?" Millie asked.

"Not yet," said Audun.

They flew higher until they were above the clouds, and when they looked down all they could see was a vast sea of puffy white. It occurred to Millie that they were higher than they'd been when trying to escape the thunderstorm on the way back from the island; going even that high had made her uneasy.

"Is this high enough?" Millie asked.

"Not yet," said Audun.

They flew until the clouds lay so far below them that they were white shapes over a background where the largest rivers were thin blue ribbons and forests were masses of green. And still they climbed until they could see the ocean sparkling far in the distance and Millie finally said, "One way or another, this is it for me. You may take after your father and be able to go to great heights, but I take after my mother and prefer seeing nice solid ground close enough to land on in less than a minute. So, if you don't mind, I'm heading back down now." Even as she talked, she was leveling out so that she could rest in a lazy glide.

"I was just about to say that we were high enough," Audun said, joining her. "We're directly above the castle now. If we tuck our wings to our sides and dive, we should be fine if we go straight. We're trying to smash this thing, not kill ourselves, so tuck your head in at the last moment. I don't want you to end up a smear on a tower roof."

"I know." Millie nodded. "And since I don't want you to be a smear anywhere, I want you to be careful, too."

Even from such a great height, Millie could sense exactly where the castle lay, so she knew that Audun was right; the castle did lie directly below them, but then so did her family, and if she missed the castle she could flatten them as well as herself, or at least leave them with a very bad memory.

"Are you ready? We won't be able to talk once we start."

"Ready," said Millie.

"Go!" shouted Audun, and they were off, their wings pressed against their sides and their legs to their bellies so they looked like arrowheads piercing the sky. They plummeted with their noses pointed directly at the castle while the wind whistled past them. And then the air grew thicker and the wind roared like a wild beast chasing them through a sky that was getting darker as the sun moved toward the horizon. A moment later they were passing through the layer of clouds and they could see the castle. It grew bigger and bigger until suddenly it was there in front of them and Audun was screaming, "Tuck your head in, Millie!"

Millie tucked her head close to her body just before she hit something that felt slightly squishy and made a loud booming sound in her ears as her momentum forced her ever lower. The next instant she was bouncing back into the sky, but when she looked down she could see a small fracture in the apparent nothingness that seemed to envelop the castle.

"Wow!" Audun shouted as he wrapped his front legs around her and they spun in circles in the air. "That was incredible! I half expected to die back there, but I never expected *that*! And did you see the rift we made in that thing?"

"But is a little crack enough?" asked Millie as they broke apart and spread their wings. "We're going to have to do it again, aren't we?"

"And I'm going with you," said a green dragon only a few shades darker than Millie.

"Mother!" said Millie. "Are you sure?"

"What you two just did is the only thing that's had any effect on Olebald's 'invisible nothing' that's keeping us out. I was appalled when I saw you diving, but I'm so proud of you for trying. If this is what it takes to get into our castle and make Olebald turn Felix back, there is nothing that could keep me from joining you. How high do we have to climb, anyway?"

"Higher than I'd ever gone before," said Millie.

Emma peered up at the darkening sky. "Then we'd best get started. The sooner I get my baby back, the happier I'll be."

This time there were three dragons climbing into the sky. Although they didn't go as high as before, it was higher than Emma liked, and she was gasping for air long before

Millie. They turned back when she could go no higher and together the dragons plummeted back to the castle. This time when they hit, the boom was louder and the crack wider, but it still was far from big enough to let them in.

"We need a lot more dragons," Audun said as they surveyed the crack that seemed to float in empty air.

"Remember how I said that I wanted a small wedding?" said Millie. "Well, I've changed my mind. I want an enormous wedding. I want you to invite all your dragon friends, and I want the wedding to be held tomorrow."

"Really?" said Audun. "If you're serious, we can send out word right away. The ice dragons would fly all night to make our wedding, but they'd fly even faster if we tell them that Olebald Wizard is here."

"Then by all means, tell them," said Emma. "I was going to ask if you were ready to make another run, but I must say that I like your idea better. I'll send word to the ice dragons and take care of the invitations to the others. I know a few fairies who love weddings, and we can round up enough bird messengers to carry the rest. Your grandmother Frazzela won't be happy to receive such short notice, and she'll be even more upset when she hears that dragons have been invited, but she loves Felix and will understand why we need to rush this. You really don't mind hurrying your wedding this way, Millie?"

"I don't mind at all," Millie said as she gazed into Audun's eyes.

"Then I have a lot to do," said Emma. "I'm glad Grassina is here. She's so good at this kind of thing. Thank you, my dears, for all your help. And congratulations! My daughter is getting married and we're going to teach Olebald Wizard a lesson all in one day. This is so exciting!"

Fifteen

Ralf and his parents were the first to arrive. When Millie spotted them, they were talking to King Limelyn, and she noticed that they'd brought Ralf's grandfather Gargle Snort, the king of the fire-breathing dragons. Millie was about to go greet them when Zoë and her family landed at the edge of the moat where everyone had gathered. No one seemed surprised to see a family of bats, however, because they were such frequent visitors to the court and everyone knew and liked them.

Zoë changed to her human form as soon as her feet touched the ground. "I'm so glad you found Felix!" she said, giving Millie a hug. "Is he all right?"

"Aside from being a tadpole, he's doing very well. Mother changed his water and he seems fine in the bowl now. Great-Aunt Grassina is holding on to the bowl until Olebald turns Felix back. We were afraid that if we set him down, someone might knock him over or drink him by mistake," she said.

"Where's your mother?" asked Li'l.

"Mother's a human again," said Millie, who hadn't bothered to change out of her dragon form. "She's with Grandfather, so just look for the biggest crowd and you'll find her."

"Thank you, sweetie. I'm so sorry we weren't here to help you with Olebald sooner," the little bat said.

"You're here now and I'm sure Mother will be happy to see you. Who is that?" she asked as a ghostly white shape emerged from the dark sky.

It was an ice dragon and Audun recognized him right away. "Frostybreath!" Audun shouted and ran to greet his friend. The two dragons met in the traditional dragon way of equals by bowing low and extending their necks along the ground. Audun had told Millie that this was a sign of respect. She'd told him that she thought it was so they could check out the opponent's vulnerable underbelly.

Millie was waiting for Audun to introduce her when a cloud of tiny fairies settled on the ground around her. Then the air sparkled and the fairies grew from thumb-sized to the size of full-grown humans. Moss, Raindrop, and Trillium were there, as well as a lot of fairies she'd known for years.

"Welcome!" Millie told them, but she knew better than to touch a fairy. Most fairies tried to avoid physical contact with dragons, even if they were the closest of acquaintances.

179

"We've come for the wedding," said the Swamp Fairy. "You know we never let ourselves get involved in the altercations of others."

"So I've heard," said Millie. "But you don't need to worry. There isn't going to be an altercation. All we have to do is get back in the castle and Olebald will have to give up. There are too many of us now for him to do anything else."

"Why is the Swamp Fairy talking to a dragon?" a voice asked in a fierce whisper, and Millie saw that Poison Ivy had also come.

"That's Princess Millie," said Raindrop. "I thought you met her already."

"Hello, Poison Ivy," said Millie. "I'm glad you were able to come." Unlike natural-born dragons, Millie didn't mind lying when the situation required it.

Poison Ivy's mouth opened in surprise. "You're Millie? I'd heard about the dragon princess, but I didn't know Millie, I mean you, were the one. Uh, it's nice to see you again."

Millie smiled her most insincere smile, certain that fairies couldn't tell the difference between one dragon smile and another. "It's nice to see you, too."

The first witch arrived a few minutes later, and soon there was a steady stream of witches and fairies setting down beside the moat. Millie wondered if Olebald was aware of their arrival or if he was sleeping through the whole thing.

It wasn't long before the largest group of dragons arrived, making enough racket that Millie was sure no one could possibly still be sleeping. King Stormclaw had come, along with four elderly dragonesses, two dozen dragon guards, and Audun's family. Millie had already met his parents and grandparents and was delighted that she was about to have the chance to meet his friends. She noticed that Song of the Glacier stayed away from the humans and gave disapproving glances when any passed by.

"There's the happy couple!" said the ice dragon king when he saw them. "I believe congratulations are in order." Millie smiled and opened her mouth to speak, but the king wasn't finished yet. "The Green Witch was just telling me about her plan."

"It was Millie's plan, actually," said Emma. "She's the one who came up with the idea to use dragon force against the 'invisible nothing' in the first place. With so many dragons here, we shouldn't have any problem breaking through the barrier. If we divide into three groups, we can take turns."

"Then we should organize now," King Stormclaw announced.

Emma was a dragon again when she organized breaking the dragons into groups. Millie and Audun were telling the last group what it needed to do when the witches Ratinki and Klorine swooped in on their magic carpets carrying the king and queen of Upper Montevista and their younger son, Bradston. Eadric hurried to speak to his parents, both of whom were scowling at the gathered dragons. Emma and Millie were in their dragon forms, so neither of them joined him.

"You did tell them that there would be dragons here, didn't you?" Millie asked her mother.

"Of course," said Emma. "I'm surprised Frazzela actually came. We'll just have to try to keep them away from the dragons, which includes us right now."

"I bet they leave early," Millie told her.

Emma smiled. "I wouldn't be surprised."

As the rays of the rising sun fanned out over the countryside, ten dragons rose into the air, including Audun, Frostybreath, and Audun's father, Speedwell. Millie watched as they beat their powerful wings and climbed until they were out of sight behind a scattering of clouds. Minutes passed and the next group readied themselves. Emma was the leader, and at her signal they followed the first group into the air.

"Look! There they are!" shouted one of the fairies, and everyone hurried to look where she was pointing.

Ten dragons plummeted toward earth like spears shot from the heavens, their wings tucked so tightly to their sides that their bodies looked wingless. They hit the "invisible nothing" with a boom that made the earth shake and the crack widen. Then Millie, Ralf, and his father, Grumble

Belly, took off with seven other dragons, racing into the sky as the second group began their descent. The two sets of dragons passed each other, but the second group was going so fast that all Millie could see were blurry shapes.

Millie's dragons had flown too high to hear the second group hit, so they climbed until she thought they had gone far enough and shouted to her companions, "Now!" As synchronized as if they had practiced for years, the dragons turned and began their descent. Once again ten dragons plunged toward earth, the cold air frosting their scales, then heating them as their speed increased. Knowing what would happen at the other end, Millie let herself fall to earth like a shooting star.

They hit with such force that the world seemed to shatter around them, but it was just the "invisible nothing" breaking under the impact of the final dragon onslaught. "Pull up!" Millie screamed when she realized that it wasn't like the last time, that there wasn't anything to cushion their fall or make them rebound.

Wings snapped open around her as she fought to spread her own, but the speed of her fall was so great that the rushing air kept pressing them closed. Arching her neck, she turned her dive into a climb; at the moment she changed direction, her wings opened so fast that it was painful. Millie angled her wings and swooped over the castle, trying to slow her momentum. She flew as far as the enchanted forest before turning back. Even then her heart was still racing and she was gasping for breath, but she wanted to make sure that all of the dragons who had flown with her were all right. Looking ahead, she saw them descend by twos and threes over the castle wall and the worry creating the knot in her stomach dissolved.

When she returned to the castle, the other dragons had already opened the drawbridge for King Limelyn's soldiers. She could hear the men's feet pounding across the wooden planks and watched them enter the courtyard with weapons drawn. They met with no resistance, however, and soon disappeared into the castle keep.

Millie searched for the only other green dragon, and when she saw her, she landed beside her mother. Emma's eyes were shining as she turned to her daughter, and a moment later they both began to change back into their human forms.

"I saw your dive," said Emma. "That was amazing! You had me worried, though. I didn't think you were going to make it for a moment."

"Neither did I," Millie admitted, running her fingers through her hair. "Have you seen Audun?"

Emma nodded. "He went into the castle with your father. There are so many people and dragons looking for Olebald that I didn't think they needed me in there as well. Apparently the ice dragons are furious with the old wizard, which is why so many of them came. They wanted to help us, especially if it meant they could get their talons on Olebald. He hurt some dragons when he escaped from their stronghold and they want him back in a bad way. I think he's in for it now. A vengeful dragon is a really nasty dragon. I doubt very much that he'll be able to get away this time."

"I hope not," said Millie. "I wouldn't want to have to deal with him ever again."

Sixteen

$\mathcal{I}$t quickly became apparent that Olebald wasn't going to be easy to find. Every floor in the castle had been searched, including the towers, and yet not one dragon, human, or fairy had seen Olebald. No one wanted to search the dungeon, however, because the ghosts were making a racket horrible enough to chill the blood of even the hardiest soul.

"I think I might know what's wrong," Millie told her mother, who was about to investigate.

"Thank you, sweetheart. I want to see how Felix is doing. Grassina asked your grandmother to hold his bowl. I just hope she hasn't put it down somewhere and forgotten where she put it. She's been doing more of that kind of thing lately."

The sound from the dungeon grew louder as Millie opened the door and stepped onto the landing at the top of the stairs. Chains rattled, doors slammed, agonized voices howled and screamed and wailed. Millie would have been frightened if she hadn't heard some of those sounds every time she'd come to visit. "What's wrong" she called, holding up her skirt with one hand whil she hurried down the stairs. "Is Hubert still stuck between the cells? Are you still trying to drown out his moaning?"

Sir Jarvis appeared at the bottom of the stairs. When he held up his hand, the clamor died away to a few dragged chains, then stopped completely. "Hubert is fine. Everything went back to normal after the castle shook for the third time this morning. It was very noisy down here, I must say. Nothing like what we made ourselves, however. No, we just wanted to get your attention. It seems we have something that doesn't belong to us, and we want to give it to you."

Millie was puzzled. "Did I leave something down here? Surely this can wait until later."

"I think not," said Sir Jarvis as he drifted to a neighboring cell. "Please take a look in here and you'll see what I mean."

Millie hurried to the door and peeked inside. As her eyes adjusted to the deeper gloom, she saw a figure huddled in the corner with its face hidden in the depths of a hood. She thought at first that it was a dead body, and she started in surprise when it moved.

"Have you come to rescue me?" asked the wavering voice of an old man.

"Rescue you from what?" Millie replied. "And who are you?"

"The ghosts! Can't you see them? They chased me n here and nearly scared me to death with that horrible creature."

Millie turned to Sir Jarvis. "What is he talking about?"

"We finally got the shadow beast under control and set him to patrolling the dungeon. He makes a marvelous watchdog. In fact, he was the one who alerted us to the old gent's presence in the dungeon. We sent the beast away when we heard the door opening just now. We thought it was some guards coming down. No need to frighten them."

"I'm glad you finally have him under control," said Millie. "This . . . What *is* your name, anyway?" she asked the old man.

"Dogsbreath," he said. "I came to ask for a charitable contribution and was trapped down here when the fire broke out."

There was something about the old man that wasn't quite right, something that made her instincts tell her not to trust him. And when he tilted his head in a way she'd seen before, Millie knew her instincts had been right. She clenched her hands, fighting the urge to turn into a dragon, wishing she hadn't come into the dungeon so unprepared.

"You must be terribly hungry," said Millie. "Come with me and I'll get you something to eat."

"That would be wonderful, miss. You're too kind." The old man struggled to his feet, pressing his hand against the damp, grimy wall to get his balance. He wore the robes of a beggar, although his speech wasn't like that of any beggar Millie had ever met. "My legs have grown numb. Please excuse my clumsiness."

He took a step toward her and lurched almost to Millie's feet. She backed away as if to let him pass, then stayed where she was as he staggered to the door.

"He's lying, Princess," Sir Jarvis whispered in her ear as the old man tottered toward the stairs.

"I thought so," said Millie. "You would have told me sooner if a stranger had been in the dungeon all this time."

"Miss!" called the old man. "Could you help me up the stairs?"

"Careful, Princess," whispered Sir Jarvis. "He's got something in his hand."

"I'm afraid I can't help you," Millie called back. "My skirts are too long and I'll need both of my hands to hold them up."

"Ah, well," said Dogsbreath. "I'm sure I can manage. It just might take me longer."

Millie peeked out the door and saw the old man take his first unsteady step up the stairs. "Take as long as you need," she told him. "I'll be right behind you." Turning her head, she whispered to Sir Jarvis, "Make sure he didn't do anything to the dungeon or leave anything behind."

The ghost gave her an exaggerated wink and nodded. "I know what you mean. We'll see to it," he said and gestured at the ghosts floating in the corridor and emerging through walls.

Millie followed the old man up the stairs, holding her skirts with both hands in case he looked back. He paused frequently, and each time he did Millie paused as well, not wanting to get any closer to him. When he finally reached the landing, he waited as if expecting Millie to open the door.

"The landing is too narrow," she told him. "You'll have to open it yourself."

Dogsbreath groaned as if the effort was too great for him, but he pushed the door open and stepped out into a sea of soldiers.

"Grab him, but be careful!" shouted Millie. "He has some kind of weapon. We'll take him to my mother and sort this all out."

"No! What are you doing? I'm not— Get your hands off me, you rogues!" cried the old man as soldiers pinned his arms to his sides and hustled him down the corridor into the Great Hall. "Why did you do this?" he yelled at Millie. "I thought you were such a nice young woman!"

"Who is this?" Emma asked as the guards deposited the old man before her.

"The ghosts found him in the dungeon," said Millie. "I think it's Olebald."

"I told you my name is Dogsbreath!"

Emma nodded at one of the soldiers, who yanked the hood off Dogsbreath's head. The frail-looking old man with tufted eyebrows and a full head of white hair gazed back at them in confusion. A murmur ran through the crowd that had gathered around to watch.

190

Millie ignored the comments and sized up the old man. "I'm sorry for asking the men to bring you here like this if you are indeed who you say you are," she told him, "but I still think you're Olebald Wizard."

"Who?" Dogsbreath asked. The guards had loosened their grip on him and he took a step closer to Emma.

"Watch out," said Millie. "I told you he has something in his hand. I think it's a weapon."

"What? Do you mean this?" Dogsbreath held up his hand, revealing a simple gray feather. "It's my good luck charm. I was afraid of the ghosts so I held it in my hand, hoping it would keep me safe."

"A weapon!" one of the guards said, and a number of them snickered, earning them a glare from Millie.

"I know one way to set this straight," said Emma. Pointing her finger at the old man she said,

> If liars never prosper
> You have to show what's true.
> We want to see your real face—
> The old one, not the new.

Dogsbreath inhaled sharply, looking horrified. Then his face seemed to grow fuzzy and vague, his features shifted, most of his hair disappeared, and Olebald stood before them. There was a rustling of fabric, and angry voices spoke out in the crowd. The human guards reached for him again.

"No!" shouted Olebald, wrenching his arms out of their grasp. The old man held up his hand. What had looked like a feather was now a knife, its tip black with what must have been poison. Waving the knife in front of him, he forced the guards to step back. And then he saw his chance and ran straight for the door.

The dragons who had been watching from the back moved in, growling deep in their throats. It was a primal sound that had terrified humans since the beginning of time. Every human in the room edged away, looking for a place to run. Even though Millie was part dragon herself, she felt her heart skip a beat.

Olebald, of course, ran faster and had almost reached the door when the dragons were on him, knocking him down, wresting the knife from his hand, and pinning him to the floor with their sharp talons. "You're not getting away from us again," said one of the dragon guards.

"Wait!" Emma shouted. "You may take him back with you, but he has to do something for me first."

The dragons hauled Olebald to his feet and dragged him in front of Emma. The old man glanced from her to the dragons, fear plain on his face. After whispering something to one of the guards, she turned to Olebald and said, "I'm surprised you went into the dungeon, considering your run-in with the ghosts the last time you were here."

"I would have left the castle, but I had unfinished business," said Olebald. "Besides, your ghosts are so stupid that they didn't even suspect it was me."

"That isn't true," said Millie. "Why do you think they kept you in that cell and sent for me? They wouldn't have done that if they'd thought you were an ordinary stranger. And what did you mean by 'unfinished business'?"

"Nothing," said the wizard, unable to meet her eyes.

"You meant to cut someone with that poisoned knife, didn't you?" Millie asked. "You would have cut me with it if I'd come close enough to you in the dungeon."

Emma gasped and turned to glare at Olebald. "You really are a despicable old man!"

Olebald's face grew red and he pursed his lips as if trying not to speak. "Your family deserves to be taken down a peg or two!" he finally blurted. "You destroyed my life, and I want to do the same to you!"

"All we did was stop you when you tried to invade Greater Greensward and take our castle from us," said Emma.

"Twice!" said Millie.

"You sent me to that horrible island with those crazy old women!" he told Emma.

"How did you escape from there, anyway?" Emma asked. "You were supposed to spend the remainder of your life on that island."

Olebald smirked. "You think you're so smart, but I have friends, you know."

"It was Nastia Nautica, wasn't it?" said Millie. "She lives close to that island."

"You took a pearl from her and she wanted you to suffer for it," he told her mother.

Emma looked shocked. "I didn't take that pearl! I gave it to her daughter, Pearl, who was supposed to give it to her."

"Well, she didn't," spat Olebald, "and Nastia Nautica has hated you ever since."

"That explains a lot," Emma murmured to herself.

"We had an agreement," said Olebald. "She'd help me leave the island and use her skills to lure the Green Witch there, and I'd get to destroy the royal family of Greater Greensward. The thought of destroying this family was the only thing that's kept me going all these years."

"It was you who planted that nasty tree in the enchanted forest," said Millie.

"That tree was supposed to drive you insane with agony," Olebald said.

Millie shuddered. "It would have if I hadn't turned into a dragon."

"And the little manticores?" asked Audun, who had finally joined them.

"They did their job. They were a distraction to get her out of the castle while I took the baby," Olebald said, scowling at Millie.

"Ah, here he is," Emma said as Grassina strode through the crowd carrying the glass bowl. Taking the bowl from her aunt, Emma cradled it in her hands and turned to Olebald. "Before you go stay with the dragons for a very long time, you have to turn Felix back into a human."

A sly smile widened the old man's lips. "I'll help you on one condition. I'll turn him back if you promise to set me free. Otherwise he'll stay a frog for the rest of his life and you'll never—"

"The only bargain you'll get is one with us," said Frostybreath, who had come in from outside and pushed his way to the front of the crowd. "You turn the baby back into a human, and we won't rip you limb from limb this very minute! We don't have any patience for you, old man, so you have five seconds to decide. One!" All the dragons in the crowd smiled, showing their fangs. "Two!" The dragons tapped their talons on the floor. "Three!" The dragons began to growl softly. "Four!" The sound of growling swelled. "Fi—"

"All right, I'll do it!" Olebald screamed.

His hands were shaking when he reached into his robes and pulled out an intricately carved gold ring. When he slipped the ring on his finger, Frostybreath leaned close and whispered, "You try any tricks and I'll rip your head off where you stand."

When the dragon placed his talons on the old man's throat, Olebald gasped and said, "I won't! I promise!"

Frostybreath snorted. "As if your promises are worth anything! Go ahead—say your spell, but be careful!"

Emma dipped her hand into the bowl. She took out the squirming tadpole and some of the water, being careful to keep her hand cupped so that the water didn't leak through her fingers. Millie noticed that the tadpole had grown little buds that would turn into legs if he remained a frog.

Olebald opened his mouth to speak. He paused and a frown wrinkled his brow. "You've got me so rattled I can't remember what I said before!" he blurted.

"Try hard," Emma said, her voice cold.

"I'm not very good at making up spells," whined Olebald.

"Just do it!" Frostybreath growled.

"I'll . . . I'll try!" Olebald whimpered. "Let me see now. Oh yes, this should work."

Turn this frog back into
The baby that he used to be.

"That's it?" Millie said when nothing happened. "I could do better than that, and I don't even have that kind of magic."

"Try again, wizard," said Emma. "And he's a tadpole, not a frog."

"All right! I will!" Olebald squeaked as Frostybreath gave him a light cuff.

This baby is a tadpole
But he was born a human.
Change him into what he was,
A human, not a tadpole.

"That was worse than the first one!" said Millie.

"But it worked," said Emma as the air around the tadpole started to sparkle. When the little creature began to stretch and grow, there was a loud gasp as everyone held their breath. The little face widened, the eyes grew bigger, his mottled skin turned pink, the leg buds grew into human baby legs and feet, and his arms and hands sprouted. Suddenly he was Felix again, pink cheeked with red gold curls and blue eyes filled with wonder.

"Oh, my little darling!" said Emma, holding him so tightly in her arms that he began to squirm and whimper.

"Now you're coming with us," said Frostybreath as his talons closed around Olebald's shoulders.

"I'd take that ring from him first if I were you," Emma told the dragon. "I'm sure that's what gave him the power to change Felix and take over the castle."

Frostybreath grunted. "I was just thinking that. Give me the ring, old man."

"But I . . . ," Olebald began. Then the dragon squeezed just a little harder, and the wizard hurriedly removed the ring and held it up for Frostybreath to take.

"You keep it," the dragon told Emma. "If we have it at the stronghold, he'll try to get out of his cell and find it. Get some rope, boys!" he shouted at the other dragons. "We're tying him up and going home. I'm sorry I can't stay for the wedding," he said, turning back to Millie, "but the king put me in charge of Olebald. You and Audun should come visit me when you can."

"We will," Millie said and gave him a kiss on the cheek.

The big dragon looked flustered from the kiss as he turned away, and his voice sounded gruffer than usual when he directed his men in tying up Olebald. The dragons marched the old wizard out of the Great Hall just as Audun and Eadric came in.

"I heard you found Olebald," said Eadric as he watched him disappear down the corridor. "What about— Ah, there's my boy!"

The baby cooed when his father took him in his arms, then grabbed a hunk of Eadric's hair in his fist and yanked.

"Ow!" Eadric exclaimed. "It looks as if he's none the worse for his experience."

"He's fine," said Emma. "I'm going to take him up to the nursery now. Grassina is handling the preparations for the wedding. Do you see her anywhere? Ah, there she is! Millie, go talk to your great-aunt. I'll be back down as soon as I can."

"Can you smell that?" Eadric asked, inhaling deeply as he accompanied Emma and Felix from the Hall. "They've started baking for the wedding. I wonder if they have anything ready yet. Perhaps we should go see."

Seventeen

illie was crossing the Hall on her way to her great-aunt when Audun matched his steps to hers.

"Believe it or not," Millie told Audun, "our wedding almost seems like a minor event after all that's happened today. I'm almost too tired to get excited about it."

They stepped aside as a group of servants carrying benches from the Great Hall walked in front of them. Other servants staggered under the weight of tables until some soldiers went to help them.

"Wait until you see what they've done to the courtyard," said Audun. "I think it looks great."

"Why are they decorating the courtyard?" asked Millie as Grassina left a group of courtiers and linked arms with her.

"Because the weather is perfect and there isn't room for everyone in the Great Hall," Grassina said. "Come outside, you two, and I'll tell you what I've planned."

Millie didn't realize how late it had gotten and was surprised to see that it was already growing dark out. The courtyard bustled with activity as fairies strung flower garlands and twinkling firefly lights between the buildings. Servants were filling bowls with even more flowers. Ralf's parents were lighting torches and King Gargle Snort of the fire dragons was already sampling fairy-made dandelion and herb wines with King Stormclaw of the ice dragons. Li'l and her children were helping the ladies of the court hang decorations from the parapets, while Garrid, Li'l's mate, helped Ralf drape banners down the sides of the towers.

"This is wonderful," said Millie, "but where are my grandparents?"

Grassina sighed. "Queen Frazzela is waiting in your grandmother Chartreuse's chamber until the ceremony begins. Eadric's mother refuses to go anywhere near a dragon, which is making things a bit difficult, I'm afraid. Your two grandfathers are directing the search for any magical traps or devices that Olebald might have set in the castle, which means that Francis and Haywood, who went with them, are really doing all the work while the two kings debate the best way to trap werewolves."

"And what is Bradston doing?" asked Millie. She had spotted her young uncle near the fairies, but he didn't seem to be doing anything.

"Ogling fairies," said Grassina. "Although he told me that he didn't trust them and would keep an eye on them for us."

Millie laughed. "That's Bradston, all right."

"It sounds as if you have everything well in hand," said Audun.

Grassina smiled and looked around with a sigh. "I believe I do, except for one thing: you. Clean clothes are waiting for you on your beds, so it's time for you to go change. Hurry now. I hear the musicians tuning up."

Millie felt more lighthearted than she had in weeks as she and Audun ran up the stairs to change. They parted at the top and Millie hurried to her chamber to see what Grassina had selected for her to wear. She had planned to get a new gown made for her wedding, but as she'd thought she'd have plenty of time, the gown had never been started. Throwing open her door, Millie ran to her bed and stopped. It was her grandmother Chartreuse's gown. Millie had seen it once when she was young, but her grandmother had told her that she wasn't allowed to touch it. Although her grandmother rarely showed affection, Millie knew that letting her wear the gown was a gesture of true love.

Millie reached out to stroke the gown with tentative fingers when one of her grandmother's ladies-in-waiting came to help her dress. The woman did her hair as well, and when Millie descended the stairs in the creamy white dress edged in pearls and decorated with pearl-outlined blossoms across the bodice, she looked and felt every inch a princess.

She had reached the corridor on the first floor when fairies arrived, bringing carefully selected flowers. It took only moments for them to weave the flowers into Millie's hair, then each one gave her a kiss on the cheek for good luck. The fairies left, and Garrid was there with his daughter, Zoë. They had brought her a necklace made of stones the exact shade of green as Millie's dragon scales. Millie bent down as her friend fastened the necklace around her throat. When she straightened up, both Zoë and Garrid gave her kisses on her cheek.

"For good luck?" Millie asked, her eyes shining.

"No, because we love you," said Zoë. "See you after the ceremony. I want to hear all about everything!"

Audun met Millie at the door leading into the courtyard. He looked so handsome in his clothes of silver and blue that her breath caught in her throat and she found she couldn't speak.

"You look beautiful," he said, raising her hand to his lips.

Millie smiled and suddenly her voice was back. "For someone who didn't know anything about kissing when we met, you've gotten very good at it."

"There's a reason for that," he said and kissed her full on the lips.

"Ahem," said her father. "I hate to interrupt, but isn't the kiss supposed to come after the ceremony? We have a courtyard full of people waiting for you two, so why don't we get started?" Taking her arm in his, he nodded to Audun and escorted Millie down the stairs.

Millie had expected to see the local pastor there to offici-ate, but she hadn't expected to see King Stormclaw waiting for her as well. It made sense, though, when she thought about it; Audun had told her that the king presided over all ice dragon weddings. She noticed that the pastor looked pale and cringed every time King Stormclaw glanced his way, but the king seemed to be enjoying himself.

Eadric walked Millie to a spot halfway between the pastor and King Stormclaw, and a moment later Audun was by her side. Although it wasn't part of the ceremony, he took her hand in his and squeezed. A warm feeling flooded through Millie; it occurred to her that she was very fortu-nate indeed to have met someone who could share both worlds with her and could understand her better than any-one else.

Lost in thoughts of Audun, Millie paid little attention to the ceremony itself. She spoke when prompted and assumed that everyone else said the right thing. But when the pastor and the king pronounced them husband and wife, and it was time to kiss Audun, Millie smiled.

After a kiss that lasted so long the guests began to fidget, Millie and Audun turned around, pausing to wave to every-one. The humans cheered and stomped their feet while the dragons roared so loudly that their breath knocked fairies from their perches on the flower garlands. The sound would have been deafening if the ceremony had been held indoors.

Millie and Audun looked out over the crowd seeing the smiling faces of their friends and family. It took a minute for

Millie to realize that one face was missing; Queen Frazzela, her grandmother, wasn't there.

"I don't think my grandmother came to the ceremony," she told Audun. "I don't see her anywhere."

"That's odd. I don't see mine, either. I wonder where they are."

Millie frowned. "I thought my grandmother might leave early, but I never thought she'd skip the ceremony altogether! I can't believe she did that!"

"I don't think she left. See, there are the witches who brought her." Audun nodded his head toward a group that included Klorine and Ratinki.

"And your grandfather is still here, so your grandmother must be, too," Millie said as she peered into the crowd. "I know they're biased against each other's kind, but I can't believe our grandmothers would fly all the way here and then not watch us get married."

"You don't suppose they ran into each other, do you?" asked Audun. "I'd hate to see what would happen if the two of them were left alone together."

"I'm sure they're fine," Millie said, although even she didn't think she sounded convincing.

The crowd thinned out as servants set food on the tables. When the guests started to sit down, Millie was pleased to see that the groups were mixed with humans sitting with fairies and dragons. She knew she should go from table to table, talking to her guests, but it didn't feel right that the grandmothers weren't there.

"I think we should go look for Frazzela and Song of the Glacier," she said, turning to Audun. "Frazzela may hate dragons, but she loves fairies and there are more than I can count here tonight. And I have this feeling . . ."

"I think you're right. Song of the Glacier wouldn't miss this unless something really important came up, but the king is here and so are the rest of his councilors."

Thinking that they could see better from the top of the stairs, Millie and Audun crossed the courtyard and started up the steps. "Millie, where are you going?" called Emma as she and Eadric hurried to meet them. "You should be out here talking to people."

"We haven't been able to find Grandmother Frazzela or Audun's grandmother Song of the Glacier. Have you seen either of them?"

Eadric had his mouth open to reply when they heard a muffled roar from inside the castle. "That sounded like my grandmother," said Audun, and they all turned to run up the stairs.

A human voice shouted, frantic and scared. As soon as they entered the corridor, a wind began dragging them toward Emma and Eadric's tower, growing louder with each step they took. They found the door to the tower standing open, and when they looked inside they saw the top half of Frazzela on the circular stairs with Song of the Glacier bending over her.

"Grandmother!" Audun shouted over the roar of the wind. "What are you doing? Leave that woman alone!"

"Don't be an idiot, boy!" Frazzela screamed. "Your grandmother is holding me up. If she lets me go I'll be sucked into this blasted hole. Help me, you fools! This poor dragoness can't hold me forever!"

Millie grabbed the door frame to keep from being dragged into the hole and tried to get a better look. Her grandmother was hanging on to the edge of a hole with her legs dangling below her. The wind was blowing around Frazzela, pulling loose items past her into the gap and creating an unearthly wail. Song of the Glacier stood with her back braced against the stairwell, straining to hold on to the old woman.

"What on earth— Mother, what happened to you?" Eadric shouted.

"I stepped on your stairs, that's what happened to me," the queen shouted back, sounding cross. "The step collapsed under me and I can't get out. Don't just stand there, help me!"

"And be quick about it!" shouted Song of the Glacier. "I can't hold her much longer."

The wind was growing stronger. Herbs that had been strewn on the floor in the Great Hall whipped past, stinging Millie's cheek when she turned her head to look.

"Olebald must have set a trap here!" Eadric shouted as he and Emma came to stand beside the hole with their arms wrapped around each other. "Audun, you lift Frazzela from that side and I'll lift from this one!" yelled Eadric. "You'll have to hold on to us, ladies, or we'll fall in, too. On the count of three. One ... Two ... Three!"

The veins stood out in Eadric's forehead as he strained to lift his mother, while Audun's face turned crimson. But no matter how hard they tried, they weren't able to get Frazzela out of the hole. Millie was afraid they were going to hurt themselves, and was relieved when they let go and stepped back.

"It's no use. We'll have to try something else!" Eadric shouted.

"Hurry up!" cried Frazzela. "I'm losing the feeling in my legs."

"Humans aren't strong enough to lift them out, but dragons might be!" yelled Millie.

Emma nodded. "Three should be enough."

It was the first time Emma had changed into a dragon in front of her mother-in-law, and the first time Millie had done it voluntarily, but Frazzela seemed more afraid of the hole than she was of any dragon. "Hurry!" was all she said as Millie reached under her arms.

The wind still felt strong, but not nearly as strong as it had when they were humans. Three dragons were able to lift the old woman out of the hole easily. When Frazzela was free, Song of the Glacier staggered back from the edge and sat down. "I must be getting old," said the dragoness. "When I was younger I could have lifted her out by myself."

"Not with that wind, Grandmother," said Audun. "You saw that it took the three of us just now."

"Thank you so much, Song," said Frazzela. "I would have died if it hadn't been for you."

"You're welcome, Frazzie. I'm glad I could help."

Millie's mouth dropped open and she glanced at Audun, who looked equally stunned.

"Take them out of here while I close this hole," Emma told Millie and Audun.

"But the wind . . . ," Millie began.

"The wind won't bother me as long as I'm a dragon. If I have to change back, your father will keep me from falling in. Now go! We're wasting time."

"You heard the dragon," said Millie as she and Audun ushered Frazzela and Song of the Glacier into the corridor. Audun ducked as a candlestick flew past, and a woman's veil came flapping down the corridor and got caught on Song of the Glacier's ridge. Millie and Audun had to work together to close the door. The moment it was shut, everything that had been flying in their direction fell to the floor, making it look as if a troop of vandals had visited the castle. The noise of the wind died down as well, although it left a ringing in Millie's ears.

"What happened in there, Grandmother?" she asked Frazzela.

The old woman looked away as if unable to meet Millie's eyes.

"We were taking a little look around," Song of the Glacier hurried to say. "Frazzie went first and the floor exploded out from under her."

"I could hardly hold on," said the old woman. "Fortunately, Song reached me before the wind got too strong or I would have been dragged into that horrid hole. Did you see how dark it was in there?"

"You have nicknames for each other?" asked Millie.

"Why not?" said Frazzela. "Song of the Glacier is the loveliest and most gracious dragon that ever lived. I'm honored to call her my friend. You know," she said, turning to the elderly dragoness, "I let only my best friends call me Frazzie."

"My grandfather can't even call her that!" Millie whispered to Audun.

"No one has ever called me 'Song' before, but I like it," said Song of the Glacier.

"May I call you Song now?" asked Audun.

"No," his grandmother said, giving him a frosty glance. "You may not."

"You know," Frazzela said, turning to the elderly dragoness, "you'll have to come visit me at Upper Montevista. We have such lovely mountains. I'm sure you'd enjoy seeing them."

"What a nice invitation! I may just take you up on that. And if I do, perhaps I'll take you for a sightseeing flight."

"Oh, I couldn't impose!" exclaimed Frazzela, although Millie thought her grandmother looked thrilled.

The two grandmothers walked away shoulder to shoulder while their grandchildren stared after them in amazement.

"You know your grandmother was covering for my grandmother," said Millie. "Frazzela was probably snooping around when she started up those stairs, and your grandmother heard her holler."

"That's probably true," Audun replied. "But Song of the Glacier would never admit it now."

"I did it," Emma said as she and Eadric came into the corridor. "I couldn't close it at first, but as soon as I put Olebald's ring on my finger, the spell worked and the hole closed right up. It was just in time, too. That wind was getting stronger by the minute. If I hadn't closed it I think it would have taken the entire castle apart stone by stone."

"I'm sure that was what Olebald wanted to happen if we were to get back into the castle," said Eadric. "I know Francis and Haywood checked our tower, but the trap was probably laid so that only a woman could set it off. We'll go over the entire castle again to make sure there aren't any more traps. However, I think we should get something to eat first. That food smells delicious. Let's go get some before it's all gone."

Emma laughed her distinctive laugh, which sounded almost like the bray of a donkey. It had been so long since Millie had heard it that she couldn't help but smile.

"You ate before the wedding," Emma protested as she and Eadric started toward the door to the courtyard. "How can you be hungry again?"

Audun waited until his in-laws walked out the door before he pulled Millie into his arms and said, "Alone at last!"

"This has been a most interesting day," Millie said, leaning against his chest. "We caught Olebald, made him change Felix back, and got married. And to top it off, my grandmother finally likes dragons!"

"And my grandmother likes your grandmother enough to offer her a ride on her back. That's the most improbable thing of all."

"This is our wedding day, so I really don't mean to argue, but I'd have to say that you're wrong about that. The most improbable thing is that you and I found each other. I thought I'd never meet the man who was right for me. Who would have thought that a human and a dragon could make such a perfect match?"

Acknowledgments

I would like to thank Victoria Wells Arms for her wisdom and patience, Caroline Abbey for all her help, and Kalissa Haff and Kitty Hamilton for their marvelous name suggestions.

Thanks also to *Wicked Plants: The Weed That Killed Lincoln's Mother & Other Botanical Atrocities* by Amy Stewart, which provided inspiration for the stinging tree. It is a very real tree that grows in Australia and a few nearby islands, with tiny "hairs" that contain a neurotoxin. Brushing against these hairs can cause unbearable pain that sometimes lasts as long as a year!

Good Book